The Christmas Kid

Also by Michael Allin

Zarafa: A Giraffe's True Story from Deep in Africa to the Heart of Paris

Thomas Dunne Books

St. Martin's Press ❦ New York

Michael Allin

The Christmas Kid

THOMAS DUNNE BOOKS.
An imprint of St. Martin's Press.

www.stmartins.com

Title page image used courtesy of Photodisc.

Lines from the poem "The Head Aim" by James Dickey reproduced by permission of the Estate of James Dickey. Copyright © Estate of James Dickey.

Book design by Victoria Kuskowski

Library of Congress Cataloging-in-Publication Data

Allin, Michael.
    The Christmas kid: a novel / by Michael Allin.—lst ed.
        p.   cm.
    ISBN 0-312-26663-4
    1. College students—Fiction. 2. Santa Claus—Fiction.
I. Title.

    PS3601.L44 C48 2001
    813'.54—dc21   2001041814

First Edition: November 2001

10   9   8   7   6   5   4   3   2   1

For Maxine Allin

The
Christmas
Kid

To be cheerful is everything.

—Sigmund Freud

1

Santa Barbara had a hot spell the week before Christmas break. While my father was back home in Kansas City shoveling snow and worrying about his chest pains, the beach at UCSB was crowded with bikinis and I was surfing all day every day, working on my cutback. I surfed even in my dreams and woke up every morning feeling the move I needed to make the cutback, muscle-hungry to get out on my board; but I never could make the move awake and for real. I could ride out anything straight into shore, but whenever I tried to attack out of headlong forward momentum and elaborate across the wave, I wiped out.

I spent that whole gorgeous week ploughing the bottom with my face and bleeding in the water. Other surfers stayed away from me, not exactly joking about my blood attracting sharks, irked at being mowed down by my relentless improvement at failure. On the beach, though, my daily wounds attracted compassionate females. Nothing makes friends like first aid. At night in the beer joints, coeds compared their deepening sunburns and marveled at how my facial scrapes and bruises matched the swirling colors of my Hawaiian shirts. My father was right to call it a country club college.

Late that Friday afternoon, the afternoon of the last day of classes for those who attended them, I was carrying my board back to the dorm, still wearing my wetsuit and holding a T-shirt to my bloody nose, when a car horn scared me and wouldn't quit. Walking chin up to stanch the bleeding, I had passed right in front of Carol without seeing her parked at the curb. I had forgotten, as usual, about meeting her and she was waiting with a vengeance. She leaned on the horn and stayed on it the whole time it took me to put my board down and hustle into the car with her.

Carol was homeward bound for the holidays and the backseat was crammed with her clothes and books, computer and printer-fax-copier and CD-tape-radio boombox, among which, secured in upright honor, rode her framed poster of walleyed Jean-Paul Sartre lighting his pipe on a bridge in Paris.

"Damn you, Casey! You told me three o'clock! You knew I wanted to be in L.A. before dark!"

"Hey, I am really, really sorry. But I'm in big trouble." My voice came out like Quasimodo through the shirt plugging my nose.

"I got your message. *'EMERGENCY! MAYDAY! SOS!'* That's why I'm sitting here two hours while you're out surfing."

"And bleeding," I tried, stoic at her insensitivity. "Won't stop."

Carol, infuriated, started the car and popped the clutch, screeching away from the curb with a whiplash that bounced my head off the seat and smashed my nose into my hand. My big brother always told me to go for the nose in a fight, and suddenly I knew what he meant; I stopped myself cold.

"I had no idea how late it was," I said when I could, leaking tears and more blood.

"You never do."

"Forgot my watch." Actually I had lost it in a recent late-night crap game with the janitors in the dorm.

"Where're we going?"

Carol stomped the brakes and I smashed my nose again.

"How about the sun going down! See it!"

"Really, I'm sorry. But I just had to get away from the tension of all the stress and the pressure you know I'm under. Which suddenly got a whole lot worse today."

"Don't you see the sun going down, Casey!"

"You're right," I said, opening the car door. "I'm nothing but bad news. I won't bother you any more. Merry Christmas."

She stomped the gas and threw me back into the seat. We circled the parking lot, going nowhere too fast. Struggling against centrifugal force, I got my seat belt fastened and tried to find my bleeding nose with the T-shirt, gingerly, but it was a painful capture.

"What happened?" Carol asked.

"Cutback. Board came up."

"No, dum-dum—your emergency."

"I've suddenly got a Lit paper due right after New Year's."

"Don't tell me you actually set foot in a class."

"Girl on the beach told me. Hit me like a bomb."

"You've got two weeks of vacation to get it done, Casey."

"What I've got is that makeup Psych midterm the day we come

back. Remember? The one my life depends on passing? I've got to cram nonstop over the holidays for it and I haven't even read the damn book for the damn paper."

"What's the book?"

"*Deliverance.* I haven't even seen the movie."

"You'll love it. It's the story of your life—an epic of survival."

The sun was setting and we kept circling into the blinding glare. Our motion flashed it off the windshields of parked cars and across the windows of the dorm. Every room seemed to be on fire.

"Carol, you are my only hope."

Hearing this, she accelerated into a violent change of direction and said, "I want to see the sunset."

I had my eyes closed when we hit the dirt path out onto the bluff overlooking the ocean. We careened and bucked, and feeling the ride was worse without seeing it, so I opened my eyes just as Carol jammed the brakes and we slid to a stop in a cloud of dust at the cliff edge. The dust sailed off the cliff without us and there it was—just another California sunset, waiting for the earthquake, with that miraculous light throwing long shadows while everything turns to gold.

"I love to see the colors come back out of the dust," Carol said and suddenly she threw the car into reverse, backed pitching over ruts, and gunned forward into another clouding slidestop at the edge. The sunset, as though seen from a cresting roller coaster, disappeared again in dust.

" 'Let the eyes.' " Carol said watching the colors come back, " 'see death say it all straight into your oncoming face.' That's from a poem by the man who wrote *Deliverance.* A poem about a person evolving back into an animal. A weasel, Casey."

"Carol, I'm on probation."

"I can't . . . I *won't* write that paper for you."

"But I'm on probation and you've read the book. If I don't pass that makeup *and* that Lit class . . . I'm history. We're talking extinct!"

"You've got two weeks."

"They'll throw me out of school! You want me to risk it? You know what my old man is threatening. I screw up one more time, he's already got the job waiting for me. Selling insurance, Carol! Call off the future, baby. Evolution goes on without me. I'm back in the mud, flop."

"Casey, you can do it. You can do it all. Your problem is why *don't* you do it? Good God, you read! You read more than I do. But nothing you're supposed to. You're like a mad scientist, the way you get obsessed with stuff and turn yourself into this . . . this . . . *useless expert* . . . on things that have nothing to do with your classes."

"I get interested."

"Why can't you get interested in not flunking out of college? Please tell me, for example, what the hell good it does you right now to know all about parrot smuggling?"

"Parrot smuggling is a lucrative and exotic faraway profession for when I crap out of college. I'll send you some lovebirds."

"That's your other problem," Carol said, stomping the car again into reverse, bouncing us faster, farther this time.

"What's my other problem?"

"Useless expert and smart-ass."

She revved into first and floored it. The tires spun dust until sudden traction launched us toward Japan.

"Lovebirds, shit," Carol muttered to herself and hit the brakes too hard. Books flew between the front bucket seats and we locked into a slide, skewing blind in a dirt version of my surfing wipeouts. I waited for airborne silence and a floating roller-coaster drop out of the dust, but we stopped.

While Carol bitterly studied the reemerging sunset, I picked up her books and, turning to replace them in the backseat, found myself facing Sartre's walleyed stare. I wondered how his walleye worked, if what it saw confused him or if he ignored it or adapted and learned ways to make it a useful liability, like a periscope that gave him a simultaneous other look at things. Did Sartre's walleye view secretly explain his existentialism? My father once described a client's overly creative insurance claim as *"moral strabismus."* I wondered if Sartre could cheat at cards with a wraparound look at what other players were holding.

Poor Carol. I had been stringing her along for weeks, in truly desperate even though self-inflicted need of her help, but keeping it platonic. Her motives, on the other hand, were as romantically ulterior as mine were selfish. We had a good thing going, nice and tacit. Until now. This was the first time she had ever refused me. So, besides needing that paper on *Deliverance,* there was the momentarily more important challenge of getting her to want to do it.

"Carol," I said with a sigh, "you've saved my life so many times. Who is it that says if you save somebody's life, it belongs to you?"

"Cannibals."

I sighed again, pathetic, baiting for sympathy. Carol wasn't having any. I held the T-shirt out to display all the Rorschach bloodblots on it while ostensibly looking for a clean spot with which to check if my hemorrhage had stopped. Carol paid no attention. My wetsuit had me sweating like a sauna.

Brain racing, I looked out to sea at the sunset and caught a new moon low on the horizon, just a faintest, lopsided jack-o'-lantern's grin, barely visible now in the dying fire colors. Some first stars were out and I searched for one I knew. It was that time of evening, that time of deepening dark below and fading light above when the stars are suddenly there the next time you look. There was no star I knew, though, and the next time I looked the new moon was gone. Carol looked at her watch and started the car. I was circling the drain, accelerating down to my last resort. She grabbed the gearshift and I put my hand on hers to stop her.

"What about you and me, Carol?"

Carol looked at me, eyes wide, mouth ajar, afraid to believe that she had heard it. I felt bad seeing how seriously she was taking it, as though her most hopeless Christmas wish were coming true, but I told myself it was this or sell insurance in Kansas City.

"Us," I said, moving in to kiss her for the first time, a long soft one.

"Oh, Casey," she whispered on my lips. I pulled away a little and she sat motionless, holding her breath with her eyes closed and her face still lifted to mine. The sunset reddened her with a healthy glow she didn't really have, pale as she was from studying all the time. Even in the Christmas heat of California, she wore her customary XXXL black turtleneck that hid everything but her intellectuality. Her only personal adornment was her hair, the color of which she constantly changed according to her insomnia. This evening, last week's peroxided orange had been purpled. I tried to run my hand through her hair, but it was so coarse my fingers snagged, and trying to extricate them revealed a muddle of past colors. The light picked up some green I remembered from before Thanksgiving.

Then suddenly Carol opened her eyes and took my face in her hands and attacked with voracious kisses of her own. Behind her, in glimpses through her hair entangling my hand, Sartre's main eye stared at me.

"Oh, Casey, Casey, what took you so long?"

"I'm going to flunk out of school."

"You're not going to flunk out. Not if you get off these tangents of yours and aim your energy at your classes. Do the work you're supposed to and just keep up. *Just . . . keep . . . up.*"

"I know, I know. I'm working on it. But I don't have the discipline that you do. I try to keep up, but I keep running out of time. And if I flunk out . . . *when* I flunk out . . . I didn't want to start something with you and then have to . . . have to lose you."

"Lose me? Couldn't you tell how I feel about you? All this time?"

I moved in cheek to cheek and whispered in her ear, "But what's going to happen to us?"

"It's happening."

"I mean, what's going to happen to us with you here and me yanked back to Kansas City, selling insurance?"

"Don't let that happen, Casey."

"Selling insurance," I repeated. And at the thought of my father's threat, I kissed Carol passionately, with no mercy.

"You'd better get going," I said, kissing her.

She answered without taking her mouth off mine, "It's a long drive in the dark. Maybe I ought to leave in the morning, huh?"

"At least we'd have tonight."

"Will you please stop worrying?" She took my face in her hands again and looked into my eyes. "Please?"

"Will you please help me out with that paper?"

Carol tilted her head and gave me what she thought was a knowing seductive grin. "Is that all you want from me?"

I commenced kissing her neck. She lifted her chin and on my lips I could feel the goose bumps I was giving her.

"One condition," she said.

"Anything."

"A solemn vow. Make me a solemn vow."

"Anything."

"You will at least read the book."

"I will, I promise, tomorrow on the plane home."

"That gives us eighteen hours." She backed the car and peeled out for the dorms. "Your place or mine?"

2

I talked Carol into a delaying detour for wine, and along with it we bought candles, bread and cheese, fruit, and doughnuts and bagels for the morning. Escape looked hopeless until we drove up to the dorm in the dark and I, Casey Rickert, the Wizard, master of the brilliant recovery, spotted Roger Woolsey.

"Damn," I said as we came to a stop.

"What's the matter?"

"I forgot I promised Roger Woolsey I'd have dinner with him tonight. He's dropping out of school."

"Roger's dropping out?"

"His father went bankrupt. Happened overnight."

"Oh, no. Can't he get some emergency financial aid?"

"They need him at home. Poor guy. He won't be coming back after Christmas."

Roger Woolsey stepped off the curb in front of us and I hit the horn. Roger jumped, startled a couple of feet in the air, and I waved, rolled down the window, and yelled, "Be right with you, Roger!" Getting out of the car, I said to Carol, "I'll tell him I can't make it. Poor guy."

"Wait," Carol said.

I waited. Roger stood peering into the dark at us, not yet recognizing who had honked and yelled at him. Carol saw the confused look on his face and shook her head.

"You can't do that to him," she said.

"No, I guess I shouldn't let him down."

"You can't."

Roger called out, "That you, Rickert?"

I answered over the top of the car, voice calm, hands desperately beseeching, "Hang on just a second, will you please, Roger?" I leaned back in through the window to say to Carol, "Damn."

"I'll wait for you."

"No," I said too quickly.

"You don't want me to?"

"I mean, I'll probably be so late. Roger's real down about it all, needs to talk, you know."

"I don't mind. I'll take my laptop to the library and write your paper."

"You don't have to do that. You've got two weeks."

I winked at her to turn this into a joke. Carol raised the automatic window tight to my throat, imprisoning my head inside the car while she revved the engine and threatened to pop the clutch.

"You don't want me to wait for you?"

"Of course, I do. You know I do."

She tilted her head with that grin again and said, "Meet you back here and you can show me your gratitude later. You show me yours and I'll show you mine."

She lowered the window and released me. As I backed away blowing her a kiss, I knew the Wizard could deal with the future in the future. If I ducked Carol and didn't show up, that already gave me another, easier problem to talk my way out of later. I didn't have to come back to the dorm that night. I didn't have to do anything or be anywhere until my plane left the next day. I put my arm around poor old waiting Roger's shoulders and walked him back toward the dorm.

"Roger, you are my only hope."

"What the hell are you up to now, Rickert?"

"Beer. On me. Your car."

That set him off declaiming, *"With sail set for the far shore of Hell, across the River of Sadness and Affliction, my vessel awaits you!"* Roger was a Lit major.

3

I took my board upstairs to my dorm room and shed my steaming wetsuit, peeling it off me inside out like the snake I knew I was. Transformed in my lucky pair of faded and shredded-to-ideal Levi's, with my favorite and most beautifully ragged Hawaiian shirt over my talismanic T-shirt from Stroud's (emblazoned across the back with the Kansas City restaurant's proud motto: *We Choke Our Own Chickens*), I was back outside and on the road with Roger inside of five minutes. The paper bag that served as my briefcase rode on the floor between my perfectly beat-up cowboy boots. Roger did not know it yet, but we were on a mission.

I had him drive down into Santa Barbara. We had trouble finding the Latino bar that Manny Ramirez had told me about; it was just a little sidestreet hole-in-the-dark without a sign or a window or anything that looked like a public entrance. We circled the block searching for it until I happened to catch a glimpse of dim light inside a closing door.

"Oh, Lord," Roger muttered as we stepped inside and headed for an empty space at the bar.

The place was dark and full of men speaking Spanish, all drinking the same brand of beer and waiting to play pool. There was no music and there was no television. There were no women and there were no glasses on the bar, only a great many beer bottles, each man holding the one he was working on with his empties mustered before him. Definitely not a college crowd, and Roger and I got looked over as we stood there.

The bartender was busy hammering a long nail through bottle caps, stacking them one by one up the shaft of the nail before sliding them off into a pile of others already with holes. Without a word or a look from us, he brought us two bottles of the only beer he served and took our bottle caps back to his hammering. Roger was nervous. We clinked bottles and drank.

"Of all the beer joints in all the world," Roger said, "here we are in the Doom Room."

"Abandon all hope and ready for worse."

"I've already got one foot running."

"Relax. You're with the Wizard."

"All the more reason to worry."

Trying to ignore the looks we were getting, we leaned against the bar and watched the pool players. They were playing for beers, winner holding the table. The winner who was now holding the table had held it for a long time; he was so falling-down drunk he literally could not let go of it. Beer bottles, his winnings, most of them empty but many unopened, covered a table and the seat of a chair. I counted nineteen. Other men stood or sat around with cues, drinking and waiting their turn to play, mumbling bored disgust while the winner staggered around the table making shot after shot.

Roger, watching him, said to me, "Another Wizard."

The winner missed. The others cheered and the place buzzed alive as the challenger stepped up to the table, carefully sought out and lined up his first shot, missed. The others groaned.

The winner took a swig of beer, slowly and carefully found the floor with the bottom of the bottle and left it balanced there, then lurched into position addressing the cue ball and, shaking his head and blinking hard to focus his eyes, recommenced to run the table.

A shoving match broke out between the challenger and his tormentors. Tables and chairs crashed and falling bottles shattered as witnesses scattered away from a knife. All eyes, except those of the winner, who was obliviously setting up for a shot, were on the two men facing each other, one with the knife, one with a pool cue. In the silence there was the woody clink of the winner's cue on the cue ball, the sharper click of the cue ball striking, another ball thudding into a pocket.

"¡SEÑORES!" the bartender shouted.

All eyes, including the winner's, turned and saw the pistol-gripped short-barreled shotgun that the bartender was aiming at the combatants. This caused further scattering out of the line of fire. The man with the knife, deferring to the shotgun, whirled the knife closed and traded it to the bartender for a broom with which he went to work sweeping broken glass as chairs and tables were righted.

Roger let out his breath and put his beer down on the bar. "Let's go, Wiz."

"Drink your beer," I said to him and leaned over the bar to ask the bartender, "Manny Ramirez around?"

The bartender did not answer, did not even look at me. He replaced the shotgun out of sight and lifted a pink plastic Christmas tree, about two feet tall, onto the bar.

Thinking he had not heard me, I knocked on the bar to get his attention and raised my voice. "Manny Ramirez?"

"You see him?" the bartender grumped, waving a hand around the bar. He began tying pieces of string through the holes in his bottle caps and tying the bottle caps onto the branches of the little pink Christmas tree.

"Manny told me you had a game."

The bartender nodded toward the pool table, "Take a stick. Winner plays, loser pays. Juanito passes out anytime now."

"No, the other game. Manny told me to tell you he sent me."

"Four dollars for your beers," the bartender said, inviting us to leave.

I reached into my paper bag and separated my cash from my plane ticket home, withdrew the cash so the bartender could see it, and laid a ten-dollar bill on the bar.

"Keep the change," I told him.

Roger also saw the wad of bills in my hand and quickly, instinctively looked around to see who else was seeing it, as a man overboard looks for approaching fins.

The bartender beamed a big friendly smile at me and slid my ten off the bar into his pocket. One of his front teeth was solid gold. "You the college kid."

"Manny told you."

"Manny Ramirez." The bartender nodded, smiling, and his gold tooth gleamed tiny flashes of reflected light.

"Can I get in the game?"

The bartender shrugged, the gesture implying that I would not be interested. "It's just some friends get together," he said.

"Yeah, Manny told me. Just friends."

"Just friends." The bartender nodded, ending the conversation. He went back to ornamenting the plastic tree with bottle caps.

Roger grabbed my arm and said, close, "Casey, please, let's get the hell out of here."

But I slapped another ten on the bar and called to the bartender, "Two more beers, *por favor*."

The bartender came back with the beers, again happily flashing his gold tooth at me. He slid the second ten into his pocket and again went back to his tree, from where he subtly directed my attention to a door in the back wall of the bar.

"Rickert," Roger said, "you are absolutely stark raving suicidal crazy to play poker in a place like this."

"I hear it's a hot table."

"It'll be hot for you, all right. Unless you lose. If you win, you're dead. Or worse."

"Lay a feel on my luggage here, *amigo*."

Roger felt my paper bag and involuntarily jerked his hand away, startled by the hardness of the .38 I was packing.

"Holy Christ, crazy ain't the word for you!"

"Nobody's going to bother me. ¿*Comprende*? Want to get in the game?"

"No way, Jose." Roger took a long pull on one of his beers to steady himself and gagged on it. "I'm hoping they'll just take my car and my clothes and let me walk home gladly naked."

"Do me a favor, if you see Carol."

"You have some famous last words, Wiz?"

"If you see her, please don't be surprised that you are quitting school because of your father's sudden bankruptcy."

"You're like quicksand, Rickert."

"Ready for worse."

We shook hands.

"Thanks for the beer and the gas."

"Merry Christmas, Roger."

Roger hesitated, reluctant to leave me there. "You're sure you want to do this?"

"*Adios.*"

Roger strode to the door and out as purposefully as he could without running.

I, carrying my paper bag under one arm and a beer in each hand, headed the other way into the back room.

4

Three hours later, six cards into a hand of high-low seven card stud, betting each card before the next was dealt, they tapped the Wizard out. My cards being obviously too good to fold, and it being such a friendly game, they let me draw light to call the bet on the last card. My hand looked sure to be low winner. They played cash only, no chips, and I figured my half of the pot to be at least two hundred dollars, enough of a recovery to buy my Hawaiian shirt back off the player who was now wearing it. When everybody turned that last card over, however, I owed thirty-seven dollars. Not a lot of money, not even two dollars for every year of my life, but I did not have it.

I did not have a watch or any rings. The only property I had to give them was the .38. This caused a furiously escalating argument in Spanish between the two winners of the pot, during which they each pulled out pistols of their own to show why neither of them wanted mine. The argument got louder and hotter, all in Spanish and incomprehensible to me, then suddenly erupted into a fistfight. The other cardplayers pulled the two winners apart and made them cut the cards to decide which of them had to take my .38.

When the loser saw his card he whirled and grabbed my ear and backed me up against the wall. He twisted my ear and his other hand was a raised fist that suddenly held a switchblade. I started crying, begging, pulling my pockets inside out to show I had nothing else. He said something to me in Spanish and raised the knife and I believe the bastard really would have cut off my ear if the others had not found my plane ticket in time.

He waited, knife to my ear, while the destination of the ticket was established and its value estimated, then, without letting go of my ear, he lowered the knife to my fly.

The others fell silent, watching. No one said a word or made a move to stop him. The bastard poked me with the point of the blade and spoke some Spanish that made the others laugh. I clenched my eyes shut and the tears poured down my face. He jabbed me again, harder, scaring a yelp out of me, and the others laughed again. He wrung my ear and knocked my head back hard against the wall before he let go and sliced both outsticking pockets off my lucky Levi's. Then he and some of the others picked me up and the man wearing my Hawaiian shirt at least opened the door before they threw me out of that back room. They kept my .38.

From the floor where I landed I looked up at the bartender grinning his gold tooth at me over the bar. On the bar beside him the little pink plastic Christmas tree was now ready for the holidays, decorated with bottle caps and a snowfall of popcorn. Drinkers and two new pool players watched me drag myself to my feet. On my way out I saw Juanito sprawled asleep on the floor under the pool table.

5

I ran. Spooked by the neighborhood, I tried to look like a casual jogger as I passed people on the sidewalk or out on their lawns cooling off, some watering their gardens in the warm night. Latin music came from open windows everywhere and whole families in all their generations sat outside their houses.

Rounding a corner I ducked behind a car to hide from a crowd in the street ahead, men and women shouting Spanish out in front of a small house. A man on the roof of the house bellowed down at the crowd. It looked and sounded like a rioting lynch mob had treed the man on the roof and they were screaming for his blood. It was terrifying until the house was suddenly illuminated with tangled strings of Christmas lights to cheers and applause from the haranging crowd, to whom the man on the roof, having found the one loose bulb, raised his fist in triumph.

I ran all the way to the lights of State Street and down it to the intersection where the coast highway and the railroad tracks curve into town from the south. I stuck out my thumb at the few passing cars, but none stopped. I considered walking while I hitched, but it was at least five miles back up to campus and mainly I did not want to leave the light, so I stayed at the intersection.

A train horn wailed far away down the coast. I heard it again and again every few seconds, blowing warnings, coming up fast through Montecito. I knew because my father hates trains—they remind him of my grandfather's romanticized horror stories of riding the rails during the Depression—and because the one time Mom and Dad came out to visit me at UCSB, I advised them to stay in Montecito: hotel overlooking the beach, lots of trees and grass and gardens and, unknown to me then, right next to that long straight stretch of highballing track.

My father told me he heard the first train coming in a dream, which was bad enough because it meant he was dreaming about his father's life in the Depression. You hear them coming from a long way down that straight track, horn blaring nearer at every crossing, then the rumbling louder and louder, so much louder you can't believe it can be coming that close but still it keeps on coming, and my father's dream turned into a nightmare about a train running over him. He woke just as the full volume of it crashed through their room, so loud my father said he could not *hear* his life flash before his eyes. Mom had to give him Valium, but by the time he got back to sleep another train roared through and it was like that all night long. My folks cut short their visit and went home the next day.

My father is an ardent amateur etymologist. Whenever he is hypothetically shipwrecked, planecrashed, stormbound, or otherwise marooned and surviving alone with a single book of choice, he takes his trusty dictionary. His old friend, Webster, he calls it.

A most honored member of our family, older than I am, Webster is one of those giant library dictionaries on a stand, a pedestal that serves as both altar and pulpit for my old man. Woe to the child who ever laid unpermitted, unwashed hands on Webster. My father loves and reads Webster daily, as he says, for the stories of the words. Also because he is addicted to crossword puzzles, the harder and more time-consuming the better. He stands at Webster fighting them for hours, sometimes off and on for days, with a faraway blind stare and his lips moving in silent search, lost in his reveries of alphabetical combination.

My father is good at being alone. Even his livelihood, studying actuarial tables and customizing life insurance to suit his clients, is for the most part a solitary activity. It has always been a wonder to me, embittered with envious resentment as I got older, how my father's proclivity for solitude could result, on the one hand, in something so practical as his ability to provide well for his family while gifting him, on the other hand, with something so seemingly unrelated, so impressive and unique, as his amazing vocabulary. And it is not just words at his command; he gets going on derivations and shades of meaning and the evolution of usage etc., etc., like a magician pulling out that endless handkerchief. I read a lot, but I can't even open a book without getting lonely. My most important study-aid has always been my Walkman.

Besides his vocabulary, my father is a nut on the Old West, especially the early woodsmen and then the later mountain men who saw the other side of everywhere first, trapping fur and fighting their way through bloodthirsty Redmen and man-killing beasts, blazing trails across the continent and opening up the savage paradise, outshooting, outriding, outdrinking, and outlying each other.

All my life I remember listening with my big brother to our father's stories about the mountain men. On driving trips or camping trips or sitting around the kitchen table or in front of the fireplace at home, Dad always told us the same stories. Whenever we protested with too-oft-heard, not-again groans, he would confess that there was something in the story he had always left out before, something he could not tell us until now, now that we were old enough. He always regained our interest that way and kept us on the edges of our seats.

The older Davy and I got, the grislier and more grimly fateful our father's stories became, like a movie you have seen over and over in black and white turning into color to reveal the terrifying reality of all that blood—Crockett massacred with Bowie and the handful of outnumbered defenders at the Alamo; Smith crawling at last to water and killed by Comanches as he lay drinking; Carson widowed with two baby daughters and the youngest dying of burns after falling into a kettle of boiling soap; brawls between mountain men fought "to the last eye"; tales of frostbitten gangrene, self-amputation, cannibalism by starving mountain men of their own body parts and of their deceased companions—and over the years the stories evolved into family discussions and after-dinner seminars on the ethics of survival, which, when Davy went away to college and later when he got married, devolved into wrangling contests between my father and me.

My father is passionate about his heroes. He quarrels with them and about them as though they were members of his own family, which they would all be if he had enough children. He named his firstborn David Crockett Rickert, and seven years later he saddled his second son, me, with Kit Carson. Only the geriatric wing of our family and a few Kansas City old-timers still call me Kit. I hated the name when I was little—other kids teased it into Kitty—so Davy dubbed me K. C., which became Casey, which became my official spelling when I went away, far away, all the way west to college on the beach in California.

My father and I used to argue about everything, anything. It drove my mother crazy. After Davy died, though, my father and I quit arguing because it got so heated and too personal. We started saying things to each other that had us apologizing later. Then even our apologies turned into quarrels. My father and I always tend to escalate. We used to kid each other out of it—even if I never won the argument, I could always make him laugh—but now we pussy-foot around each other trying not very successfully just to get along. Losing Davy wrecked us.

6

Headlights came at last around the curve, slowed into the light at the intersection, and the car stopped for me. The passenger door opened for me, but I was suddenly paralyzed seeing two Latinos in the front seat. I should have known from the car, a Chevy more than ten years old, immaculate and shining with a thousand pounds of customized chrome.

"Get in, man," the passenger said, sliding close to the driver to make room for me.

"Thanks anyway. I'm going all the way to Goleta."

"We go Goleta, man. Get in."

At this moment a powerful headlamp swept across the highway and the train I had been hearing rumbled slowly around the curve into town.

The driver of the Chevy leaned in front of the passenger to yell at me, "Hey, *'mano,* you want to ride or no?"

"Sorry," I said.

I closed the door for them with great care and the Chevy purred away slower than walking speed up State Street. I would describe that Chevy now as beloved. That night, though, after what had just happened to me in the bar, the way the car gleamed and disappeared around the corner at rolling idle was nothing but evil creeping death on its way back to get me. I was sure those two guys were circling the block to avenge the insult of my refusal to ride with them.

The train was a long freight, slow boxcar after boxcar. A single empty flatcar went by with a guy riding on it, then more boxcars, then a string of flatcars with no end in sight. Paranoid about that Chevy, I walked closer to the passing train to see how I felt about jumping a flatcar.

It was easy, they were going by so slow. I sat on my flatcar and watched the lights at the intersection float away behind me into the night and wondered why I had never jumped a train before. It was wonderful. Hell, I thought, I could ride the rails clear back to Kansas City and my folks would be none the wiser. It would be cold, but I could bundle up in my surfing wetsuit. I lay on my back and looked up at the stars. I found Orion. Telephone poles and treetops flowed by on either side and Orion seemed to be moving along with me, over me. I would be all right. The Wizard was back on the road and bound for glory.

Orion and I rolled through town and, after the wear and tear of events, the movement and the slow clattering rhythm of the wheels on the tracks felt good. Goleta was only five miles up the coast, but I didn't want to think about Carol waiting for me. I closed my eyes and told myself to keep thinking positively, to think about Fred.

Her mother named her Frederica and called her Ricky. Her father called her Fred. Her parents split up when she was twelve. She loved her mother and adored her father. She understood and accepted their divorce, after living through their emotional crash and burn, as the best thing for everyone concerned. But she never forgave her mother's family for how badly they kept on treating her father.

Fred's mother comes from old money, and they made every hell they could for the ex-husband. They tried to drive him out of sight, out of mind, out of business, out of town. He stuck through it all and stayed in Kansas City to be close to his daughter. He stayed in their faces and she grew up loving to prick their pretensions. When her mother's family and their connections snubbed him out of the Kansas City Country Club, my father sponsored him into Mission Hills, where we belonged. That made Fred a member of both clubs and she spent her teenage summers packing the quieter, genteel pool at the Club with her rowdy friends from Mission Hills.

After the divorce, no one but her mother and her mother's family and their Club friends called her Ricky. Her mother would always introduce her as Ricky the Daughter; and Ricky the Daughter would take each new person's hand and smile into their eyes and ask them please to call her Fred. Then when she said good-bye to them, if she had decided that they were just another of what she called her mother's fools, she would give them her hand again with the same sweet smile and ask them please to call her Ricky. She still does it now, all grown up, with her mother's drop-dead manners and her father's guts.

The issue of her name is just one of many running skirmishes in Fred's lifelong war with her mother's family. She inflicted them with her major coup when she named her baby Matt after her father. And she loves what she calls the poetic vengeance of the fact that she and her son both have her father's unforgettable wild red hair.

"Aim for the chip on their shoulder," Fred always says, "and salt their wounds."

I do not remember ever meeting Fred. I do not remember a time when I did not know her. She and Davy were the same age and I was always her kid brother, too. I was forever hanging around Davy, driving him more or less crazy, but he usually stuck up for me with the older kids. Fred *always* stuck up for me, even against Davy, even when I was a pest. Until she was ten or eleven, she was bigger and tougher than most of the boys her age. I fell in love with her long before Davy did, ever since the day she rescued me from our local bully and beat the bejesus out of him. When Davy found out about it, he went and beat the kid up all over again.

In later years I always joked with them that looking out for me had brought them together. When they started going steady in high school, Fred made Davy take me with them everywhere they went. Because her father was so mercilessly ostracized by his former family and friends and in his business, Fred was fierce and unforgiving about Davy and me, brothers, sticking together. It was you and whoever loved you against the world, or please call me Ricky.

Little Matt was born the summer I turned thirteen. That Halloween night the four of us went to Stroud's for the country-fried chicken that is really only an excuse to overdose on the mashed potatoes and thick country gravy. The mashed potatoes look like piled-high clouds, taste with the gravy like heaven, and fill you so full it feels like you'll never be hungry again. Leaving Stroud's, you feel like you own the world and have just eaten it.

Stroud's was filled that night with people we knew in costumes, crowding the bar and eating at tables, fortifying themselves for a private party at the Club. Little Matt lay in his car seat on our table with all the food, fascinated silent by the bizarrely dressed creatures who stopped by to say hello and try out their repertoires of baby-greeting grimaces and funny noises.

Driving home, Fred wanted to crash the party. I volunteered to baby-sit so she and Davy could go. Davy said it would be a snore. Fred insisted; Davy resisted; I was enlisted to accompany Fred. Davy dropped us off at the Club, but they would not admit us to the party because we were not in costume.

We were standing at the open door of the ballroom, rebuffed, listening to the music and identifying various dancers in their disguises, when Fred recognized Marie Antoinette's décolletage as that of her mother.

"There's the old lady," Fred said, "stooping to conquer."

Suddenly Fred pulled me by my arm to the door of the ladies' room. I balked at the entrance—an open doorway with a louvered standing screen obscuring the interior—but Fred yanked me in around the screen with her.

The ladies' room was empty, but I remained terrified that some gossipy hag from the upper echelons of Kansas City society would walk in. For as long as I lived and longer, as long as old ladies were alive to remember and remind, people would point me out or merely hear the name Rickert and recount scurrilously embellished versions of what I was doing in there that night. It was the kind of circumstantial evidence that creates a lifelong inescapable and humiliating nickname, an early epitaph I would wear all my years.

Along with my fear of discovery, though, I was surprised at how posh the ladies' room was: the expanse of deep-pile red carpet, coordinating floral wallpaper, white wicker easy chairs, white wicker chaise lounge on which Fred emptied the entire contents of the big leather mailbag that, all these years later, is still her purse.

Fred rummaged stirring through the tangled clanking mass of different perfumes, diapers, lipsticks, batteries, wallet, sundry aerosols, giant jar of Vaseline, baby wipes, baby powder, baby bottle, baby clothes, makeup, flashlight, several pairs of sunglasses, winter gloves, passport, black lace brassiere, address book, notebook, Dr. Spock's baby book broken into two sections and loose pages, loose pills and keys and pens and money, coins and bills—one of which was a forgotten hundred-dollar bill she was amazed and excited to find and celebrated by kissing me—hair equipment and worlds of other items and clues to her life that I could not identify, all mixed up with escaped crayons and baby toys and rattles and nipples and pacifiers and what had to be a lifetime supply of Tampax.

I was thirteen years old, alone with a grown-up female whom I adored in, of all places, the ladies' room, *the War Room—BEHIND THE LINES!*—of the Kansas City Country Club, for the first time in my life looking upon the mystery of what a woman carries in her purse. My mother's purse has always been off-limits to me. She told me when I was little that every woman carries a snake inside her purse, guarding her privacy.

Fred's, however, was humbling enlightenment. Revelation. Over the years since that night I have come to think of it as a conceptual model of how life in the universe keeps going. Women keep it going. As though the universe is this infinite purse in which everything is not exactly lost, and every woman carries around her own microcosmic bit of it.

Fred, with her purse, was ready for anything. I count my experience with her that night as my first and most precious intimate moment with a woman. In my memory it surpasses even the mystery and intensity, and certainly the fearful fun of a subsequent, never-to-be-forgotten, never-to-be-repeated summer night with Betty Flanagan under a blanket in a sand trap on the seventeenth hole of the Mission Hills Country Club.

Making a separate pile of her hair equipment—brushes, combs, cans of spray, tubes of mousse—Fred directed me to wet my hair and sit myself down on the red carpet. She got down on her knees with me and began squeezing tubes, discovering that we were mousse-poor but Vaseline-rich, so she compensated for our lack of the former by mixing it in her hands with a big disgusting glob of the latter.

Her hands crackled as she worked it up and then, cackling ghoulishly, she massaged this reeking green extraterrestrial slime-goop into my hair. I can still feel her fingers. We laughed so hard together I got the hiccups and was secretly mortified by the ever more probable embarrassment of farting, while Fred was openly afraid that she would, as she put it, pee in her postpartum pants. Laughing too hard to stand, she crawled away through the doorway into the room where the stalls were.

"Don't leave me!" I begged her.

"Don't look in the mirror!" she warned me, laughing hysterically.

I never forget the awful glimpse of myself in the mirror over the long dressing counter—hair greased into a cyclone, laughing, choking on hiccups—and I could hear Fred peeing and laughing with me around the doorway. I was on my knees, desperately arm-flailing away the aroma of a Stroud's-inspired emanation, when a woman, I think, masked over heavy makeup and wearing a top hat and tails, entered, dancing solo around the screen. We both froze and gaped in shock at the sight of each other while Fred laughed hysterically in the next room, until Fred's toilet flushed, breaking the spell and Marlene Dietrich or Fred Astaire or whoever it was made an abrupt about-face exit.

Fred crawled back laughing through the doorway, bursting into even more uncontrollable hysterics as she saw me again and got busy combing and spraying and sculpting my hair until it was pet-rified flat and zooming straight out behind me. Fred *VELOCI-TIZED* me!

Then it was her turn and I helped Vaseline and brush and spray her long red electric hair—*"More Vaseline!"* became our rallying cry ever after that night—so it stood up and out around her head like a halo of flames.

Finished, or at least out of Vaseline, Fred put her biggest pair of sunglasses on me and gave me the flashlight.

We had no trouble infiltrating the party. Anytime anyone asked us what our costumes were supposed to be, I shined the flashlight in Fred's face and she screamed. No one got it and Fred refused to tell them.

Fred's mother avoided us, but her snooty friends kept coming up to us in their masks and elaborate costumes to ask about ours and, in answer, Fred kept screaming at my flashlight; it was the loudest human sound ever heard inside the stately old Kansas City

Country Club. After a while people asked just to hear Fred scream. The mystery dancer in top hat and tails who had found me in the ladies' room had disappeared, probably, Fred said, because she was a he seeking a little anonymous voyeur action or an old-money closet transvestite who was afraid I'd recognize him/her on the dance floor.

It was typical of Fred that instead of pissing everybody off by crashing their party, she nearly won us the prize for most original costume. Someone who was in on the voting told me later that the only reason we lost was because Fred would not divulge to anyone there that she was a screeching cat caught in the headlight of a speeding motorcyclist, me, who was about to run her over.

When Fred and I performed it, still laughing, at home for Davy, her feline death-shriek woke Matt and we heard him crying. Davy would not allow Fred to go to her wailing baby in the middle of the night looking like that. Over the years Fred and I have never stopped laughing together about that night—every Christmas since, it has been a family joke that Fred and I gift each other with giant jars of Vaseline, ingeniously disguised until unwrapped; and the smell of the stuff always brings our adventure back to me—but I have also suffered from it ever since with my worst guilty secret: I remain convinced that Fred, my big brother's wife, now his widow, is the only woman I can ever love.

7

During my reverty of remembering Fred, the slow ticking rhythm of the train put me to sleep. The next I knew the flatcar was jerking and bucking so violently I couldn't sit up, blasting along through blind dark so fast I couldn't open my eyes in the wind of it, teaching me immediately why the other guy I had seen aboard the train rode in the lee of a preceding boxcar. I was helpless to do anything but ride out the pounding, flat on my stomach, face buried in my arms.

I had no idea how long I had been asleep or where in the world I was. I could not tell how long I rode hanging on like that, bouncing and sliding around, unable to see, and every second expecting the edge of the flatcar to find me. But at last I felt the flatcar lurch into a wide curve and slow down enough so I was able to sit up.

The dark around me loomed like black thunderheads closing out the stars and I realized the train was climbing into mountains. Orion was gone. It got colder and colder as the train wound on up, grades steepening, curves tightening, and I couldn't see a thing except black mountains opening and closing a ragged flow of stars I did not know.

At any moment I felt the train was going to topple over into the screaming dive of a roller coaster. But descent, when it finally came, was the same blind winding crawl until, cold hours later, the curves opened approaching glimpses of lights spread out in the distance. The five miles I had expected to ride that train had turned into eighty, way up the coast past UCSB and over the mountains inland to San Luis Obispo.

8

It took me the rest of the night to hitchhike back over the mountains and down the coast to the campus. The sun was coming up when I finally dragged into sight of the dorm. Carol's car was one of the few left in the parking lot.

I was dead tired and all I wanted was to collapse, but opening the door of my room I saw Carol asleep on my bed wearing my robe. Her laptop sat closed on my desk, and on top of the little computer was a fresh paperback of *Deliverance* she had bought for me along with a green binder containing the paper she had written for me. Carol stirred in her sleep and I ducked back out into the hall, commandeered an abandoned room, locked the door, fell on the bed.

I was awakened once by a door slamming, but it fit into a dream I was having and I slept on. I woke up late that afternoon aching all over, starving, and saw for the first time how filthy I was and how torn up my clothes were from my ride on the flatcar. Looking at myself in a mirror, I saw why my father always hated to hear my grandfather feeding his Depression adventures of riding the rails to Davy and me. My grandfather was always the hero of his stories, but there was nothing heroic or romantic about my survival. All I saw in the mirror was someone who looked as bad as I felt.

I looked out the window to check the parking lot and was relieved to see that Carol's car was gone. In my room I found my robe on the floor and *Deliverance* on my desk, but no green binder containing the all-important paper. No food, either. Two burned-down candles were all I found of everything we had bought the night before.

I searched everywhere for that green binder while getting out of my ruined Levi's and my Stroud's T-shirt that was now a rag, then putting on my robe I found handfuls of the paper in both pockets. Carol had taken the binder with her after ripping the perfectly printed pages into irreparable shreds, which I tossed into the air and which fluttered down around me like Christmas snow, like New Year's confetti.

Except for me and the Yemeni identical twins who never spoke to anybody but each other, our entire floor was deserted. In the showers I was still swaying from the train and still so tired I sat on the floor against the wall under the water. I leaned my head back, trying not to hurt the bruise that had resulted from being slammed against the backroom wall of the bar.

The Wizard had got me way into bigdeep this time. In Kansas City the family was getting ready to go pick me up at the airport, but I had lost my plane ticket and I was flat broke. And if my father found out, he would not even give me the very good chance

I had to flunk out of college. He said I needed direction, discipline, focus, which he would supply if I did not. He would focus me right into selling insurance. Or if it were up to the old man, I would join the army. One of his favorite, most fervently held beliefs is that what America needs is the peacetime draft. He is convinced that compulsory military service, with no wars to fight and die in, is the perfect way to knock what he calls *"the taurine fecal matter"* out of young men in general and out of me in particular.

I sat under the shower with everything hurting, still swaying with the train, trying to get clean. Some of what I thought was thicker grime would not wash off and turned out to be bruises on my forearms and thighs. The hot water stung a cut I had not seen over my left eye. My upper lip was swollen and my tongue found a new chip in one of my teeth. Suddenly Davy's chipped front tooth came back to me and I could not stop crying because you saw it whenever he opened his mouth and I had already forgotten it.

Everybody says that time heals. Time does not heal. Time only forgets. Until a memory breaks your heart all over again. I was terrified of forgetting Davy, terrified of suddenly remembering him.

I tried to think what Davy would do to get out of my trouble. Davy. The good son. My big brother, the rescuer who never needed rescuing. Davy never got into my kind of trouble. The worst thing Davy ever did was die, and even that was an accident.

All I had left of Davy was Fred and their little boy Matt. And I wasn't there. This was our first Christmas without Davy and here I was screwing up, as usual. Worse than usual.

I tried to think and, as usual, all I could think of was to call Fred collect and ask her to credit-card a bus ticket to me. I would make it up to her. I would read *Deliverance* straight through on the bus. I would write that paper myself and cram nonstop for that midterm. I would be the hero of Christmas and cheer up the family. I would do everything I was supposed to do. I would try not to be in love with Fred. I would take Matt to see Santa Claus.

Matt was my junior partner in crime. He was seven when Davy died. After the funeral I dropped out of UCSB for the rest of the summer quarter, and Matt and I spent every day together. He didn't want to talk much, but then neither did I. We hung out a lot in the library, went swimming and to the movies; and every afternoon, unbeknownst to the family, we frequented a divey little bar I had found downtown.

The joint was known as the Whileaway, but the sign outside just said OPEN 6 A.M. Inside it was old and dark and cool, the customers mostly old-timers, neighborhood regulars who came in every afternoon to shoot pool and play cards and drink beer and lie to each other. They put Matt in charge of racking the balls and paid him in Cokes. It was like a club, with always the same faces, and they were always glad to see us. The place did us both good and Matt liked keeping it secret from the family.

Then the week before his eighth birthday Matt turned sullen. Fred and the rest of us tried to cheer him up with plans for his party, but the closer it got the angrier his indifference became. When the day came Matt didn't even want to leave the house, but I got him to go with me to the Whileaway as a favor. Matt was riding up on my shoulders when we got there and found a hand-written note taped outside saying *"closed due to repairs."*

The door was unlocked, though, and inside the place was mysteriously deserted and even darker than usual. We hit the lights and *"SURPRISE!!!"* the regulars all jumped out from hiding. Balloons drifted everywhere, full of sinking human breath instead of helium. A worn old *HAPPY NEW YEAR* banner swagged behind the bar.

The guys set Matt up at the bar while one of them locked the door, and the proprietor brought out a cupcake with a candle stuck in it and we all sang "Happy Birthday," one well-oiled old-timer singing high against the melody in perfect harmony, then holding the last note long, incredibly long after the song had ended. His face turned bright red while he held the note and the others timed him, marveling at his revelation of a skill they had no idea he possessed. Matt was openmouthed amazed by this performance on his behalf, and when the note ended after two minutes and twelve seconds, he led the ovation.

I bought beers all around, whereupon the singer, warming to the awestruck audience he had found centered around Matt, chugged his entire bottle of beer nonstop. Another man, not wanting to be outdone in Matt's eyes, grabbed the empty bottle and juggled it with two billiard balls. This inspired another old-timer to tear the Kansas City telephone book in two, then he did same to a full roll of toilet paper. Another regular deftly reversed the lit end of a cigarette into his mouth and balanced his cane on his chin while blowing smoke through his nose.

Matt sat at the bar sneaking gulps of my beer, enthralled by these extraordinary senior Olympics, applauding and cheering his head off. When the contortionist wrapped his arms around his own back and writhed in the hilariously groping passion of a lover, then stood in profile and with torturing effort seemed to swallow the entire length of a pool cue, Matt got so excited he ordered more beers for everybody. By this time I was broke, so the proprietor, as a birthday present to Matt, opened a tab for him.

With Matt's tab running, and after the oldest guy there cartwheeled up onto the bar to walk it back and forth on his hands until his false teeth fell out, the festivities turned cerebral with wit-twisting games and saloon-lore involving coins, matches, peanuts, and various magical ways of folding a napkin.

Those old-timers were wonderful to Matt, and I, of course, lost track of the time. When I finally realized how late we were, Matt invited one and all to his other party at home. The guys taunted my alarm at this idea by enthusiastically accepting.

"Sure!"

"Let's go get cake!"

"Yeah, we're party animals!"

"Is Mom good-looking?"

"Is *Grandma* good-looking?"

"We'll bring a keg!"

"Two kegs!"

"Do you have a swimming pool?"

At the mention of a swimming pool, they fell silent and looked around at each other, all getting the same idea before yelling in unison, "SKINNYDIPPING!!!"

"Who's got a car?"

This brought a sudden longer negative pause and one of them at last winked at me.

"Aw, too bad."

"Sorry, Matt."

"Yeah, nobody's got a car."

"You have fun, though."

"Have a great party, Matt."

"Thanks, guys," I said, hoisting Matt up onto my shoulders. "You're all the greatest."

"The best greatest!" Matt said. "I can't wait till next year!"

"Happy birthday, Matt!"

"Many happy returns, Matt!"

"Thanks for the blast, kiddo!"

"Bring Mom in!"

"We'll have a Mom Night, Casey!"

Matt's head was spinning from all the surreptitious beer he had drunk, and I had to carry him home. When we walked in late to his party, I was already unpopular with the family. They had gone all out with a clown-magician and the house was full of kids and parents and decorated with dozens of hovering helium Mylar dinosaurs.

Matt didn't give us away, though, until he threw up blowing out the candles on his birthday cake and my father smelled our beer breath. Then Matt defended me by drunkenly trying to convince the family that they had the wrong idea, that it had been a surprise party, the *greatest* birthday party ever with our friends who were the *greatest* bunch of old guys down at this *greatest* bar I had been taking him to every afternoon and where now he even had his own charge account.

Matt started day camp that week and I spent the rest of the summer working as an office boy for one of my father's clients.

9

I was surfing and wiped out. Suddenly I was drowning and panicked awake, but I still couldn't breathe and I couldn't see where I was. I was awake but I couldn't get out of the dream. I had dozed off in the shower and it was full of steam. My robe had fallen on the floor of the shower and was soaked so I had to hold a towel around myself, one of those goddamn little gym towels that are never big enough to fasten around your waist.

On the way back to my room I called Fred on the pay phone near the elevator, collect. I had trouble handling the phone and holding on to my towel while speaking to the operator.

Fred's recorded message answered, "Hi, this is Frederica Rickert. I'm not here right now, but *YES,* operator, I do accept collect charges from Casey Rickert."

I took my deep diver's breath and held it, waiting for the beep, but my towel slipped loose and, grabbing for it, I dropped the receiver. I pulled my towel back up and my message began with me catching the receiver swinging clunking against the wall, then I blurted out my rap seemingly in a race to get it all said before the time was up.

"Hey, it's me. Dropped the phone. Hey guys, please forgive me, but I'm going to miss the plane. I got stuck with a last-minute science assignment for extra credit, and my team pulled an all-nighter. Dissecting a human heart. Absolutely unreal. Most utterly amazing night of my life, and we're still not done. Tell Dad I really may switch to Pre-Med. And the extra credit is going to do wonders for my grade point average. I'll call you back later and work out when you'll see me. Soon as possible. Main thing is I'm all right and not to worry. Sorry. Love you. Love you, Matt!"

I went back to my room and got dressed, feeling really proud of myself for letting Matt down. Worse, I had lied to Fred. And I had put her in the position of lying to the family when I called later to confess why I needed a bus ticket. I didn't want to account to the old man for my lost plane ticket, so I would have to coordinate my arrival at home with an L.A.–K.C. flight and just show up out of the blue.

I had not eaten anything since one of the bagels Carol and I had bought the night before. The cafeteria downstairs, where I could have eaten for free on my resident's meal ticket, was closed for the holidays. There were some sandwiches and snacks left in the vending machines, but I had no money.

There was no one around the dorm so I set off outside looking for somebody I knew. In front of the dorm a uniformed chauffeur was loading luggage into the trunk of a white Mercedes limousine and as I passed I saw the identical Yemeni twins ensconced watching a television in the backseat.

I searched the campus for somebody, anybody I could hit up for eating money. I even checked out the library, setting foot inside it for the first time all year. There was no face I knew anywhere. Finding the campus bookstore open, I hustled back to the dorm and threw some of my class books into my duffel, intending to sell them. When I got back to the bookstore, though, it was closed.

I wandered off the deserted campus into the neighboring area of restaurants and stores crowded with Christmas shoppers. It was evening and the lights were coming on. Everything was decorated for Christmas and the streets were full of traffic. People jostled each other with their shopping bags on the sidewalks. It was the last Saturday before Christmas and I remember thinking shopping centers and stores were crowded like that all over America, except in Santa Barbara it was warm and people were eating at tables outside some of the restaurants.

I walked around, famished, and it struck me that every person I saw represented one Christmas dinner. I was surrounded, not by people, but by all their Christmas turkeys and hams and geese and gravy and stuffing and mashed potatoes and sweet potatoes and pumpkin pies and apple pies and cherry pies. I remembered shoveling snow for people back home after Christmas, trying to make some money, and the ladies trying to pay me instead with pieces of leftover pie. I would hold out for the money and they would give me the pie anyway. The last week of the year was the best time to shovel snow, eating pie while I walked from job to job, with the smell of Christmas trees burning out of chimneys around the neighborhood.

That night in Goleta, though, I smelled hot dogs. Outside a department store, my nose led me to a hot dog stand with a long slow line of waiting customers. I stopped and watched hot dogs being built—idiosynchratic combinations of frank, mustard, relish, onions, chile, cheese, sauerkraut—each finished product an epic of mouthwatering Americana.

As I stood there savoring aromas and rabidly drooling, a guy in a jolly fat Santa Claus suit rushed out of the department store and, checking his watch, hurried to the end of the line for a hot dog. A little kid already in line yelled for Santa to come take his place. Santa Claus thanked the kid, declining, but then everyone else insisted that Santa go first and they all had a good time pushing him to the head of the line. Waiting for his order, Santa bowed in gratitude to his benfactors, who were now an amused audience sharing the experience instead of separate and anonymous hungry people.

"All your presents are on their way," Santa announced to them. "May all your wishes come true! Every day in every way! Merry Christmas every day of the year!"

When Santa tried to pay, the proprietor refused to take his money and everyone applauded. Santa blessed the proprietor and everyone else again for their Christmas spirit, then trundled back into the department store with his free hot dog. The people still in line kept on talking and laughing together, and the woman who got the next hot dog traded holiday farewells with all the others.

Wandering hungry, lugging my duffel full of books, I passed a Nativity tableau outside a church. It amused me that one of the life-size Magi pointed across the street to a little municipal park where spotlights illuminated a life-size Santa Claus in a reindeer-drawn sleigh full of presents. My amusement became epiphany, though, when I saw that Santa's reindeer seemed to be pulling him toward an adjacent supermarket.

10

*M*oments later, I was strolling crowded cheerful aisles with a cart, wolfing pickles and Christmas cookies after a sandwich (on white bread for its facilitating softness) of an entire package of sliced salami garnished with salsa and washed down with a quart of health-conscious lowfat milk. I was chewing half a banana, cheeks puffed out like a tuba player, when I passed an aisle and made eye contact with a clerk. He was stacking cans and stopped when he saw me. I kept on going. I do not recommend bananas for speed-eating.

Turning the next aisle I started to ditch the banana peel behind cereal boxes, but the clerk's footsteps were coming fast. I only had time to toss the peel over into the next aisle before he came around the corner. I pretended not to notice him, not daring to swallow the last choking mouthful, engrossing myself in the nutritional statistics on a box of Froot Loops.

The clerk downshifted into cool and pretended to straighten

shelves. He wore a little polka-dot bow tie and an apron with *May I help You?* on it in matching polka-dot letters under his name tag that was decorated for the holidays with a sprig of plastic holly, and he had a neon chartreuse feather duster sticking up like a tail out of his back pocket.

As we both stood pretending not to notice but watching each other out of the corners of our eyes, each waiting for the other's move, somebody threw the banana peel back and it landed smack damn right on my shoulder.

I looked in amazement from the peel to the clerk and he could not believe it either. Then, outcooling the clerk with my shocked but good-natured innocence, the master of the brilliant recovery walked over to him and without a word—seemingly for silent dramatic effect, but actually because my mouth was full of stolen banana—waited for him to remove the banana peel from my shoulder. He took the peel and lifted it, dangling, like something filthy between his thumb and forefinger. I turned away and finally swallowed.

"Need a hard hat in here," I said without looking back.

I would have played it more outraged, marching out of the market in a theatrical huff, but it would have taken that clerk only seconds to find the open and the empty packages in my cart. I remained innocent as long as I stayed in the market, the legal assumption being that I intended to pay for whatever I had eaten. One step outside, though, and the clerk had me for shoplifting. Now that he knew the cart was mine, I had to get rid of the incriminating evidence. So I proceeded with my shopping.

I took my time in that aisle, not looking back until turning the corner. The clerk was still at the far end where I had left him. He was also at the far end of the next aisle, which I passed when I saw him. He was also at the far end of the next aisle. And the next. He was onto me.

I began to shop for my life, reading labels and comparing prices per item, prices per container size, prices per serving, ingredients, colors and graphics and psychologies of packaging . . . stalling . . . waiting . . . praying for unobserved seconds to stash my trash in the shelves.

But there were no unobserved seconds. Wherever I went the clerk was behind me or ahead of me. When I turned an aisle fast he was behind me *and* ahead of me. He was everywhere, with his perky bow tie and his solicitous apron with his festive name tag and his chartreuse tail feathers.

Instead of getting rid of anything, I shouldered my duffel to make room in the cart, which I loaded until it was this rolling mountain I wrestled around and around the store, careening into shelves and other shoppers.

The Wizard was desperate. I stopped to browse the magazines and paperbacks. I found a copy of *Deliverance* and read every word on the front cover. The cover was illustrated with the hand of a desperate corpse reaching up out of a river. I read the blurbs on the back cover. *"Brilliant, breathtaking . . . Stomach-churning . . . Tooth-and-claw survival . . ."*

The clerk was down the aisle, straightening bottles of grape juice into identical symmetrical ranks.

I opened *Deliverance* and read more blurbs on the first page. *". . . A primitive and violent test of manhood . . . that will curl your toes! . . ."* I read the title page, the dedication, the publishing information and history, and the one epigraph that was not in French before I looked up again.

The clerk was aligning apple juice, size by size, brand by brand, with all the other fruit juices, size by size, brand by brand, still to do.

I read the first sentence of *Deliverance*.

11

I *felt a tap* on my shoulder. Checking my place in *Deliverance,* I could not believe that I had read nearly forty pages.

I felt another tap and came up out of the book distracted and smiling into the face of the clerk. Now it was his turn not to speak to me as he knelt by my cart and summoned me with a forefinger. I knelt and the clerk pointed to a thick brown puddle on the floor under my cart, a puddle into which my cart was dripping.

"Rocky road," I said.

The clerk stood. I stood.

"Sorry about that," I said.

The clerk said nothing. He put his hands on his hips and just stood there looking at me. I showed him *Deliverance.*

"Ever read this? Wow!"

The clerk took the book. Without answering me, without even reading the title, he reshelved it with the other paperbacks. He resumed his akimbo contempt and looked at me some more.

Suddenly I felt wonderful. All my troubles disappeared in a surge of insulted righteousness. Not only for myself but for myself and for *Deliverance*. I loved that book! If it had not been a class assignment and I had found it before on my own, I would have already reread it several times along with all of the author's other work, including everything I could find out about his life and how he got that way, immersing myself so deep in the project that, for a while, I would actually *be* James Dickey. It is a chameleon-habit of my mind, like having multiple personalities who all try in turn to rectify but only worsen the trouble I get myself into; like being all the characters in my own movie, and usually it's a horror film.

The clerk smirked at me and I smirked back at him, hard. I reached around behind him and reclaimed *Deliverance,* secured it among my groceries and shoved on with my cart dripping a trail of liquified rocky road ice cream down the aisle.

Bottles and cans and cartons of fruit juice now stood in perfectly repeated rows, glimpses of infinity. I remember suddenly wondering if that was why military parades marched in lockstep unison, and if that was the psychological significance of uniforms—to imply infinite anonymous and invincible numbers of soldiers, police, parking ticketers, janitors, mailmen, firemen, tuxedos and mink coats, doctors and nurses and brides and housepainters and ice cream vendors in white, cheerleaders, athletes, cowboys—*grocery clerks!*—all marching to civilization's battle against chaos and AWOL flakes like me.

Looking back at the clerk, who was still watching me, I pulled a bottle of the largest family-size prune juice off a shelf and put a hole in the perfection of his work. There were only two women shopping in the aisle, both with that preoccupied faraway look my father gets doing crossword puzzles, and I managed to crash into both their carts.

I muscled my cart around into the next aisle. Akimbo Superclerk was there, now overtly blocking the other end. I stopped, trapped.

An old lady came up behind the clerk and spoke to him. The clerk answered her without looking away from me. The old lady did not hear the clerk and/or she did not like his manners, because she raised her cane and tapped his arm with it until he turned to face her.

No prior intention, nothing but sheer reflex made me lob that prune juice over the shelves into the aisle I had just left—an overhead hook shot to where I knew it wouldn't hit anybody. There was a loud wet-heavy shattering explosion overlapped by a woman's scream overlapped by another woman's scream.

The clerk, also in reflex action, darted back around his end of the aisle toward my diversion. The old lady followed her cane after him. I grabbed *Deliverance* and took off for the exit.

The market already had cops outside waiting to nab me, but hearing the screams the cops rushed in and I slipped out across the parking lot into the dark of the adjacent park.

I dove with my duffel into bushes just as sirens arrived and more police cars screeched into the parking lot. I lay in the bushes and watched shoppers and employees being evacuated from the market while the cops organized an aisle-to-aisle search for me. I saw them questioning Superclerk.

I had the shakes so bad I couldn't stand and had to crawl away out of the bushes. In the last twenty-four hours I had lost every cent I had, more than I had, on a dumb-ass poker hand; had got myself relieved at knifepoint of my plane ticket home for Christmas; ditto my .38, now probably being used in some rampaging multistate crime spree with my fingerprints on it; had almost got an ear cut off; had almost killed myself on an eighty-mile midnight roller-coaster ride to San Luis Obispo; had promised and reneged on sexual favors to cheat my way clear of flunking out of college, hurting a sweet loyal friend who would be spending her holidays sticking pins in the eyes of a stuffed monkey she had named after me; had got myself hunted by police for shoplifting and assault with a bottle of prune juice; had let Matt down; had lied to Fred.

I crawled to a tree and sat against it, reeling in a panic through all my screwups, each one spinning into another like a nightmare I have all the time—always different but the same, variations on a theme—where I am trapped in a maze of those distorting funhouse mirrors that ripple and twist people into monsters. Every way out turns into another mirror and I keep banging into these hideous versions of myself. People love those mirrors. They love to see and laugh at themselves as mutant freaks, I guess because it convinces them that they are not mutant freaks. Other people are. It's like kids playing in a wheelchair they can walk away from, or like watching the news at eleven to see what catastrophes did not happen to you today. Today, though, the news was all about me. And it was all bad.

UCSB campus cops arrived at the market. I was wearing my UCSB sweatshirt, inside out as always for luck, but Superclerk's description of me would be as precise as his rows of fruit juice. I didn't dare go back to the dorm or even show my face on the streets, and it wouldn't be long before the cops might sweep the park looking for me.

Brain racing, circling the drain yet again, I saw Santa Claus in his sleigh.

I was on the dark side of the sleigh, the park side hidden from the street, and it was no problem just to ease the mannequin slowly out unnoticed and drag it away into the dark. I stripped off the red suit and put it on with the stocking cap and the white beard. I buried the naked mannequin in a Dumpster full of grass cuttings.

I stepped with my duffel to the curb in full Santa Claus regalia and raised my thumb to oncoming headlights, and all hell broke loose. Vehicles traveling in both directions immediately started honking at me, and drivers and passengers of all ages waved and shouted Christmas greetings, Hanukkah greetings, jokes, taunts, encouragement.

As I stood there waving back famously, not daring to look around at the police activity half a block away, a siren whooped behind me. I raised my hands in instinctive surrender, turned, and saw the UCSB cops saluting me as they passed northbound toward campus. Out the window of their backseat came a thumbs-up from none other than Superclerk.

12

I had no idea what I was getting into, but the Santa Claus suit seemed to have its own luck and I was all out of mine. I had witnessed the public goodwill, the mob generosity, and the free hot dog that the other Santa had inspired; but I knew nothing at all yet of the suit's real power to save me for bigger and better danger. The world around the Santa Claus suit is like a dreamworld where you know no one—as usual, the street is full of passing strangers—but everyone knows you. You become a target for how people feel about Santa Claus. And some of them, I would soon learn, never forgive you for not existing.

The car that stopped for me was a Mercedes convertible, shining new without plates, top down blasting rock and roll to the world at large, lone driver silhouetted against the flurries of passing headlights. Expecting to ride up front I tossed my duffel into the backseat and had the door open before I saw that the figure behind the wheel was a teenage couple glommed together.

"Symbiotic Siamese twins, joined at the telephone" was my father's constant description of Davy and Fred going steady in high school. My father concluded that those symptoms of teenage senility otherwise known as puberty—he listed them once in a letter about me to Davy as *"phylogenic body hair and voice change, rapacious interest in the opposite sex with concomitantly increasing shoe size, dermatological volcanics, and auditory deterioration with respect to parental frequencies"*—are all onset and kept on track by daily hours of sustained pressure to the adolescent ear from a telephone receiver.

The two teenagers in the Mercedes were in what my father categorizes as the symbiotic Siamese automotive mode, dangerous but preferable, he feels, to the endless busy signals of the telephonic mode. The girl rode fastened inside the boy's right arm, her left elbow nestling in his groin, her arm on his thigh, her hand down somewhere in the dark between his knees.

I followed my duffel into the backseat and we were off in a cloud of hormones. I was Santa Claus, suddenly ensconced in VIP posh.

The girl lowered the radio, turned her wild hair and laughing eyes at me, and said, "You're not like a mass murderer or something, are you, Santa?"

"Not if you've been good," I said.

"Ho, ho, ho," she said, returning forward to ask the boy, "I've been good, haven't I?"

The car ran so quietly that even in the backseat with the top down and the music low I could hear her fingernails strumming the inseam of his jeans, a snaking rasp that set my teeth on edge.

"Real good," she teased him.

"Don't ask your mom," the boy said, changing lanes with that left-arm mastery that you do not learn in Driver's Ed. "You headed for L.A.?" he asked me in the rearview.

Where else for weird? Who was it that said the continent is tilted so everything *loose* slides to L.A.? My father. But I have caught him quoting without attribution; when called on it his standard reply is that great minds work alike.

"Kansas City," I heard myself say.

"Kansas City!" Hair whirled and wide eyes were back on me. "Hitchhiking?"

"Home for Christmas."

"Kansas City's, like, all the way across the country!"

"Only halfway. Halfway and a little more."

"How many miles?"

"Sixteen hundred."

"How far to Chicago?" the boy asked.

"Two thousand," I said to his eyes in the rearview.

"How long will it take you?" the girl asked.

"Eighteen hours to Santa Fe, fourteen more to KC, morning after tomorrow."

"All that way so fast? No."

"Straight through," the boy explained to her, then to me, "I've been to Chicago."

"Without stopping?" she asked me, checking her boyfriend's road lingo.

"I turn left down at Ventura and the sun comes up in Arizona. I turn left again at Albuquerque and the sun goes down. I turn right in the night out the top of New Mexico and the sun comes up in Kansas and when Kansas ends, I'm home."

"All that way!" The girl could not get over me. "Santa Claus . . . *hitchhiking*! What a concept! Thanksgiving, you could be a big hitchhiking turkey. And a big bunny at Easter."

"What a concept," I agreed.

"You're so cute!" she said. "What other holidays are there? Let's see . . . Oh, I just love road games! Now . . ."

"Actually I didn't think of it," I confessed. "I was already on the road and won this outfit in a poker game."

"Santa plays strip poker!" the girl giggled with an in-joke laugh to the boy. Visions of road games danced in my head.

"Not hardly," I said. "Not in a truck stop. Last thing you'd ever imagine is a bunch of truckers playing strip poker. Be like Marines dancing with each other."

"Why are Marines always so short?" the girl asked, rhetorically, because no one answered.

I went on, "Anyway, it got so cold up north I put this thing on. Right away it was ride after ride nonstop, cars lining up for me, drivers arguing over me, even trying to outbid each other for my company. Talk about your commercialization of Christmas. They offered me money in front of their children."

"Long rides?" the boy asked.

"I had to turn down meals."

"What's your longest ride so far?"

"Coos Bay–Obispo in a semi."

"Wow," he said to the girl, impressed.

"New Year's!" the girl burst out, brainstorming on the sly. "You can wear a diaper and be, you know, the New Year's baby?"

I said to the boy's eyes in the rearview, "Driver fell asleep at the wheel and we went offroad in the middle of the night."

"Wow."

"Seventy-five mile an hour, headed like a train straight at a farmhouse."

"You like crashed?" she asked.

"What happened?" he asked.

"Colossal U-turn. Through a pasture scattering milk cows. Udders flopping in the headlights. Made a complete circle around the farmhouse. Driver double-clutching, downshifting, spinning the steering wheel, working like a one-man band to keep the rig from jackknifing or sinking into the ground."

"Why didn't you just, you know, *stop*?"

"Farmer started shooting at us from his upstairs. The house was dark, but on the way around gunfire flashed out the windows and shotgun pellets rained like hell all over us."

"But you missed the house," the boy said.

"Just caught a corner of the porch. Fishtailed through a chicken coop, though, and set loose every feather on the place. The most spectacular worst was the greenhouse. I'll never forget the sound of all that glass shattering. I know I'm going to hear it in my nightmares. We took two clotheslines full of sheets and longjohns with us back across the pasture, slaloming to re-avoid bovine panic. Smashed through the fence again and back out onto the highway. After that, the driver decided to stick to the back roads and I got out."

"Wow!"

"What's bovine panic?"

"Cows, babe," the boy explained. "Wow!"

"How do you like the Benz?" I asked him.

The girl said, "My mom just got it, to celebrate her latest divorce."

"I got a ride with a cowboy who rodeos out of one of these. Hundred thousand miles a year hauling a two-horse trailer painted to match. Set of longhorns for a hood ornament."

"Ever been to Chicago?" the boy asked.

And on down the coast while I got their story. Heather was already late when she and Randy picked me up in her mother's brand-new Mercedes-Benz. They were close to home and Heather was supposed to be driving. Heather was also supposed to have been at her study group cramming to retake the SAT. Heather was going to college. Heather was grounded for everything, everything meaning Randy, until after she had retaken the SAT. Heather had taken the SAT once and needed to bring up her scores because her grades were not so hot.

Randy's scores and grades were not much better, but basketball was Randy's ace in the hole. In fact, Ace in the Hole, shortened to Ace, was what the coach and the team and Heather and their whole high school and even the local newspaper called Randy. Representatives of several institutions of higher learning had approached Randy with basketball scholarships, all contingent, of course, upon Randy's academic and playing eligibility, both of which were taken care of by the coach. The coach was like a father to Randy.

After being approached with one particularly prestigious basketball scholarship, Randy was found celebrating with Heather in her room. Heather's single mother approached the coach and pled for her daughter's future, with the result that Randy's college career was now also contingent upon Randy staying away from Heather. Another result was the rumor going around about

Heather's mother and the coach, who was married. Randy did not believe the rumor about Heather's mother and the coach, but Heather was not so sure.

Heather and Randy were a couple of screwups after my own heart. They were already into and risking even more serious trouble, but they decided to drive me all the way to Ventura and my first left turn. It was only an hour out of their way, round-trip. An hour was no problem for Heather to explain to her mother. Neither Heather nor Randy realized, and I did not mention, that the sixty miles on the odometer might incriminate her explanation. We rolled untroubled through the mild California night, trading stories of star-crossed love, comforted by body-molding leather and quadraphonic rock and roll.

13

outh of Montecito the highway winds along the ocean, so close I could see phosphorus spark the waves as they rose to break in an avalanche of glowing surf. I have never been to Key West, but I read everything I can find about it and dream all the time of getting down there—another of what Carol calls my aimless obsessions.

I should not have gone on and on to Randy about working on the shrimp boat out of Key West and tending bar on Caroline Street and living with the girl who sang in the bar and who owned a fifty-year-old blue macaw named Luigi. Every night was a party in the bar and we always slept past noon. Luigi woke us every afternoon with operatic arias, which he sang in the magnificent tenor voice of my girl's beloved deceased singing instructor. Key West is the southernmost piece of America, 375 miles farther south than Cairo, Egypt, and 90 miles north of Cuba. Summers get so hot there that the shrimpers sweat off their tattoos. The best time was the month around the autumnal equinox, after the worst heat and before the worst tourists—hurricane season. Key West is situated right in the middle of Hurricane Alley, vulnerable to Gulf, Atlantic, and Caribbean storms. After a hurricane Key West was a paradise of rainbows. There were rainbows everywhere, wherever you looked, of all sizes: rainbows in raindrops caught in spiderwebs; rainbows laced amid steaming frangipani, festooning the dripping branches of the ceiba tree (source of kapok), the strangler figs, the screw pines, the wishbone cactus; neigborhood rainbows reaching from block to block of the little town; transoceanic rainbows arcing over the entire island with one end out in the Atlantic and the other end out in the Gulf of Mexico. Puddles reflected rainbows in scattered pieces all over the streets. The sunlight, that blazing stormlight after a hurricane, was so amazingly, miraculously beautiful, with the air so clear and clean, that every time you saw it was like seeing things and pure colors again for the first time. My girl rode her bicycle up Duval Street under the rainbows, splashing through the rainbows with Luigi on her handlebars. Luigi was a bicycle expert, spreading his brilliant turquoise and yellow-flashing wings wide, wider than the handlebars for balance, yellow-breasting proudly into the wind in front of my girl and belting out Pagliacci. When hurricane season ended the tourists came and carried Luigi's fame back with them. Only Hemingway was a more renowned denizen of Key West. Hemingway had known and loved Luigi in the old days and had taught him a bawdy little Spanish ditty that Luigi still screeched full blast exactly as he had learned it in Hemingway's voice. But only at dawn; and as a result the old-time conchs, the born-and-bred native Key Westers, would swear they had heard Papa's ghost singing the sun up again. One night while my girl and I were away at work, robbers broke into our beach shack and kidnapped Luigi. When we came home feathers still floated in the air. Luigi had put up a fight. For heartbroken days my girl and I collected every feather and added them to the others we had always so carefully saved and never sold, not one, no matter how much the tourists offered. We searched the island, listening desperately for the slightest wisp of familiar melody, grieving, tormented by sudden false hopes from radios and the whole panoply of contemporary electronic musical reproduction. We couldn't eat. We couldn't sleep. One morning at dawn, lying weeping together in our hammock, we thought we heard Hemingway. Then we heard Pagliccai and Luigi flew in through the leeward window clutching in one talon what we discovered was a human ear. It was a left ear, savagely amputated with streamers of ripped flesh caked with the same blood that stained Luigi's powerful black beak and the black and yellow feathers of his throat. Ecstatic as he was to see us, Luigi refused to relinquish his gory trophy, viciously defending it from our attempts to take it away from him while he stood on it and ate it in shreds. We suspected transients, but kept an eye out from then on for a local van Gogh. After that came the star-crossed part of the story. My girl had a hit record and chose her career over me and Luigi. Randy and Heather knew her music. She became a household name. Luigi died of missing her. I buried him at sea and cast our fortune of his collected feathers to the Gulf Stream.

Heather was crying. She had turned off the quadraphonic rock and roll during my story and, now in the silence, as Luigi's feathers drifted floating away toward Europe, Randy pounded the steering wheel with his driving fist.

"I'm so sick of school," he announced, "I'm going to postpone college and hit the road. See some *life*!"

"What about your scholarship?" Heather asked.

"Basketball will wait for the Ace."

"What about me? I'm supposed to go to college alone?"

"You'll have more time to get your grades up."

This sent Heather furiously out from under Randy's arm and into her own bucket seat, saying, "You're no rocket scientist either, you know! Scholarships like yours don't grow on trees . . . Gorilla Boy. Tell him, Santa."

"You've got to go with your gift," I tried, wincing in my beard at my tone of wise old Coach Santa. "Most people aren't so lucky to have one. That's why there are more fans in the stands than players on the court."

All I had wanted was to escape the cops, but here I was changing this kid's life. Whatever the source of my power—the Santa Claus suit itself, or what a cool hustle these kids thought it was— my effect on Randy was alarming. I could and should have tried the truth on him; could and should have yanked off the white beard and confessed that my stories were only the wishful lies of a terminal daydreamer. But at the moment that seemed like spitting in the gasoline after dropping the match, because my truth quickly became irrelevant to the escalating lovers' quarrel I had ignited.

"And please tell me, thank you very much, what do you expect me to do while you're off God knows where doing who knows what!"

"It'll be football season. You'll have the entire team to keep you company."

"And what'll you do without your cheerleaders? You know you're addicted to pom-poms!"

"Listen to little Miss Flirtbucket!"

"Gorilla Boy!"

When we arrived at my turn in Ventura, Randy still had both hands on the wheel and none of us were speaking. Randy pulled over and stopped at the curb a little before the intersection. I got out with my duffel.

"Thanks, guys, for going so far out of your way."

"See you in Key West!"

"Try college first, Randy. 'Bye, Heather. Merry Christmas."

"Yeah. You have a nice life, too, Santa."

I jaywalked behind the Mercedes as it pulled out into the left-turn lane and stopped to wait at the light. I had no intention of hitchhiking. There was a pay phone on the eastbound corner and I was going to call Fred and go Greyhound.

I was waiting for the collect operator when the stoplight changed and the Mercedes U-turned north. Randy honked. I waved, suddenly in the high beams of a California Highway Patrol car roaring straight at me, scaring the hell out of me, and I dropped the phone to raise my hands.

The CHP howled past me all lit up, flashing colored lights, and tailgated the Mercedes to an immediate stop in high beams and spotlights. Both front CHP doors opened and, using the doors for cover, the cops emerged drawing their guns, aiming over the doors at Randy. Red lights flashed forward in the white halogen glare hitting the Mercedes, orange flashed back on me in the dark, and smaller blue to the sides flickered over each cop.

I picked up the receiver and drifted into the shadow of the

phone booth, not wanting to be seen, also not wanting to be seen hiding as the passenger cop held a radio mike in his other hand and a loud piercing amplified voice commanded, "HEATHER TUTTLE! HEATHER . . . TUTTLE! ARE YOU FREE AND ABLE TO EXIT THE VEHICLE! HEATHER TUTTLE, INDICATE IF YOU ARE FREE AND ABLE TO EXIT THE VEHICLE!"

Heather appeared waving over the headrest, blinded by the white light, yelling that she was all right.

"DRIVER, STAY WHERE YOU ARE! DO NOT MOVE, DRIVER! KEEP BOTH HANDS ON THE STEERING WHEEL! HEATHER TUTTLE, YOU WILL NOW PLEASE EXIT THE VE-HICLE! NOW, HEATHER!"

Heather stumbled out barefoot. She held up a hand against the light, both hands against it, crossed her arms against it in front of her eyes. The red lights pulsed on and off her.

"COME BACK HERE, HEATHER."

Heather staggered out of the white glare, out of the throbbing red. When she was within reach, the passenger cop pulled her into the blue light, into cover behind him. The blue flicker made it seem as though she was underwater with the cop.

"DRIVER, LISTEN CAREFULLY! DO NOTHING UNTIL I TELL YOU TO! WHEN I TELL YOU TO, YOU WILL EXIT THE VEHICLE! SLOWLY! WITH YOUR HANDS OVER YOUR HEAD! AFTER YOU HAVE EXITED THE VEHICLE, SLOWLY, WITH YOUR HANDS OVER YOUR HEAD, YOU WILL LIE DOWN ON THE GROUND! FACEDOWN ON THE GROUND! DRIVER, YOU WILL NOW EXIT THE VEHICLE! LET'S GO, DRIVER!"

Randy came out, tall, long arms up high as though defending

the basket and, like Heather, blinded by the light and disoriented. He approached the CHP car and both cops instantly tensed, straight-arming their weapons at him.

The amplified voice bellowed, "DOWN!!! GET DOWN!!! ON YOUR FACE!!! DO IT!!!" and Heather was screaming, "Don't shoot! Don't shoot! He's my boyfriend! My boyfriend! My mother hates him!" and Randy scrambled down flat on his face on the highway beside the Mercedes. Those cops certainly went all out for a single mother with a new car and a wayward daughter. The good news was that Randy's future looked like it was safely out of his hands for a while.

As Randy lay there, a pickup turned my corner and slowed to honk at me. I waved back at the driver, whose face was shadowed by a baseball cap. I started to remake my call. The driver of the pickup leaned out into the streetlight and shouted to me, "Merry Xmas, Santa!" She was so pretty my thumb flew up and the pickup jammed to a stop. I hung up the phone and threw my duffel into the truck bed and got in with Sharon.

14

"N ice beard," Sharon said.

"Forgot I had it on, sorry."

"No, leave it on."

"Yeah?"

"I love beards."

"How far you going?"

"My family has an avocado ranch here in the valley."

"We've got a lot in common."

"We do?"

"You like beards and I like guacamole."

Away from the coast the freeway that entered the valley narrowed to highway, and the valley narrowed, deepening between mountains dark with orchards. Sharon told me it was avocado up there. Your avocado, she told me, does better than your citrus on the higher slopes. The dense groves along the road were some avocado, but mostly orange and lemon. Your citrus, Sharon told me, likes it better lower where it's warmer. My citrus certainly did, I agreed, and after that we had each other laughing all the way. She was around Fred's age, this or that side of thirty. Divorced, she said.

Deeper into the valley the highway narrowed to two-lane. Solid walls of dark trees closed in on both sides under a winding river of stars. Sharon rolled down her window. It was warmer than the coast. I rolled down my window and smelled oranges in December. At Sharon's turn I accepted her offer of something to eat and the use of her phone.

Two turns took us up a steep twisting dirt road between trees so close that branches slapped and clung and leaves whisked and unseen avocados clunked the pickup. I learned why Sharon rolled up her window when a cannonball concealed in foliage sprang in on my side and conked my ear. As we bushwhacked up through the musical avocado car wash, Sharon explained that she could tell when her "rascals" were ripe for picking by the descending tone and decreasing reverberation of their impact on her windshield. *Clunk . . . clonk . . . clonth.*

"As with most things, *splat* is way late," I offered.

"Not for guacamole."

"Any wild animals up here?"

Sharon stopped the pickup in the trees, killed the engine and the lights, and rolled down her window. I rolled down my window and we sat listening to the dark.

Within moments, something big rustled off in the leaves on my side.

"Critter," Sharon said.

I rolled my window up fast as Sharon, laughing, fired the engine and the lights and drove on up the mountain.

"We stay out of the trees at night," she said.

The pickup jounced out of the trees into a clearing at the top of the mountain. An Australian shepherd ran barking in and out of the headlights as they swept across the ranch house and buildings, all dark. We got out and the dog jumped all over Sharon, whimpering beside himself to see her. I took my duffel and followed them in the dark toward the house.

We were up high. The mountaintop was a dark island in a black sea of treetops. A cottonwood tree stood tall and spreading over the house, this time of year an immense leafless tangle full of stars. The stars seemed to scatter out of it like sparks across the sky. I saw one fall in a long streak erasing itself.

When Sharon turned on a light that showed me how well her Levi's fit her, I suddenly felt as happy as the dog. I followed her through a mudroom that was like a secondhand shoe store displaying different varieties and huge-to-tiny sizes of galoshes and Wellingtons and workboots and cowboy boots and sabots and running shoes and old street shoes used for gardening, with similarly various coats and hats and weather gear hanging on pegs around the walls. The mudroom led into a kitchen, where a marmalade-colored cat named Marmalade rubbed figure eights around and between Sharon's legs.

The dog, seeing my Santa Claus outfit in the light in the kitchen, froze into a menaced crouch and stared at me. One unblinking eye was brown, the other milky blue.

"It's OK, fella. C'mon, fella," I said, slapping my leg to call him friendly to me.

The dog growled at me low in his throat. That blue eye scared me. The brown eye was a good dog's eye, deep dark, gleaming; but the blue one was flat, icy white, with nothing in it but a black needlepoint of pupil.

I appealed to the brown eye, "Easy, fella . . . easy . . ." and asked Sharon, "What's his name?"

"Killer!" she yelled at him. "Knock it off, Killer! Get over here."

Killer slunk over in front of Sharon and froze on me again, growling louder, protecting her.

"Killer!" Sharon poked him with her foot, causing him to snarl teeth at me. "Killer!!!" She poked him harder and he seemed to change shape, hackles bristling him bigger, ears flattening and streamlining his head into relentless eyes and snarling fangs aimed at me. The cat arched hissing at the dog.

"Hey, Killer. Good Killer. Hey, good Killer," I said, trying not to look in his blue eye.

"It's the beard," Sharon said.

I took off the beard and Killer's eyes followed it as I dropped it on the floor for him to scent. He tensed forward, stretching out low to sniff it, keeping just out of nose's reach of it. His ears rose and his gray-mottled body relaxed and rose forward over his nose as he olfactorized the mystery. Then he turned to lift a hind leg and sign off on the beard, but Sharon cursed him away in time. She picked up the beard and flicked it at him. Killer, retreating, snapped at it. Sharon whacked him with the beard and threw it on a counter. Killer went and lay down against a far wall and kept his different eyes on me.

I let out my breath. "Whew."

Sharon laughed. "Takes one to know one."

"One what?"

"Killer's crazier than a shithouse rat sometimes. You must be, too." She looked from me to Killer and yelled affectionately at him, "Weird-ass!"

"That one blue eye is spooky. Which I guess is the same way he feels about Santa Claus."

"You think it's just the Santa Claus suit, huh?" She grinned from Killer to me. "Weird-ass."

We had the house to ourselves. I hoped when Sharon took off the baseball cap that her dark hair would cascade long and shining over her shoulders and down her back. Her hair went nowhere, though. It was short with shaggy bangs that stood up when she tousled her cap-itch, tomboy gorgeous. She gave me a bottle of wine to open while she brought out an enormous leftover ham and a carving knife.

We sat at the kitchen table, taking turns with the carving knife slicing pieces off the ham, eating with our fingers. It was a delicious smoked ham glazed with mustard and honey, salty and sweet and it tasted like I would never get enough of it. The wine was white, spicy, in a longnecked bottle with a German tongue-twister of a name that Sharon hilariously tried to teach me and I hilariously failed to learn to pronounce.

The cat jumped up on the table and joined us, accepting morsels from both of us. I offered a piece of ham to Killer. He stayed where he was, unbuyable, eyeing me without raising his chin off the floor. Sharon threw him a piece that he caught in his teeth and swallowed without chewing.

The cat eventually quit and Sharon and I slowed down on the ham, now and then slicing one more last bite for each other. I got enough of the ham, but I could not get enough of the sheer delicious taste of it. I wanted to keep tasting it even after I was stuffed.

Sharon and I sat talking, finishing the first bottle of wine and opening another, both of us scratching the cat, who closed its eyes and hunkered into a purring sphinx on the table between us. I forgot about Killer. Sharon tried again to teach me how to say the name of the wine, but with all we had drunk and our laughing, she became as unable as I was to pronounce it. Our fingers touched in the cat's fur. I took hold of Sharon's fingers to emphasize a joke, at which she laughed so hard that she pulled away from me to hold on to the table. While she laughed I waited for her fingers to come back to the cat. When they did I took hold of her again. She started to pull away, laughing again, but I held on to her. She stopped laughing and gave me a little amused smile. She turned my hand over to read my palm, and her fingernail traced my lifeline, tingling electric, long and slow, like the arc of that falling star. I moved in to kiss her. Killer growled. I froze looking into Sharon's eyes. She grinned.

"Coward," she said.

Resuming toward her I heard Killer's claws click on the Spanish tile as he stood up to growl more seriously at me. I refroze, inches from her lips.

Sharon laughed in my face and pulled her fingers out of mine. She finished her wine and, refilling her glass, said, "Killer was on to you the minute you walked in the door." She drank and said, "So was I."

"Don't you believe in Santa Claus?"

"Not since I was nine, when I sat on his lap and felt what he wanted to give me for Christmas."

"That was a vile imposter. Shame on him."

"And what are you?"

I picked up the carving knife, cut off a piece of ham, tossed it to Killer, and kissed Sharon. In seconds Killer gulped the ham and interrupted me with a snarl. I cut off a much bigger chunk that I thought would take Killer some time to chew, threw it to him, and kissed Sharon nowhere near properly before he threatened me again.

"Hell," Sharon said.

She stood, picked up the whole remainder of the ham, and led Killer out of the kitchen with it through the mudroom, where she opened the door and hurled the ham out into the night. Killer tore outside after it. Sharon slammed the door, marched back into the kitchen straight to my Santa Claus beard, and put it on.

Back at the table, she stood over me. She took my face in her hands, leaned close, looked down into my eyes. We were both wine-and-tired bleary. Looking up at her like that made me dizzy. Her eyes were green, and under and around her eyes freckles floated among laugh lines. I couldn't focus on the freckles and laugh lines and with my dizziness they reminded me of the stars I had seen whirling out of the cottonwood tree.

She opened her legs and sat straddling my lap. I felt the beard on the side of my face and her breath in my ear as she whispered, low and slowly, provocatively drawing it out, *"Gewurztraminer."* Then she picked up the bottle of it that was still alive, took my hand and pulled me to my feet and, bearded and wine-bearing, she led me blind through the dark house to a bedroom.

15

The bedroom was so dark my eyes never adjusted and I stayed blind in a wine-whirl of escaping clothes and tangling arms that were legs, legs that were arms and shoulders finding knees and sudden hands and lost mouths and breathing that sometimes caught sound in our throats.

Through it all I did not see a thing—kept whirling back awake to her and could not tell in the dark if my eyes were open or closed—until car lights swept like double lighthouse beams through the bedroom window. All I saw then was a disappearing flash of Sharon over me with her head thrown back so there was nothing of her face, only the Santa Claus beard she was wearing and my own hands covering her breasts.

Blindness returned and my hands emptied. Sharon, panicking off me, stomped me in the stomach with a knee. I could not see and I could not breathe.

"Shit!" I heard Sharon hiss in a frightened whisper over near the window. "You've got to get out of here! Fast!"

Something hit me in the face. My fingers found the beard. I jumped up, putting it on in contagious panic.

"Who is it?" I asked.

"My husband!"

"You said you were divorced!"

"He'll kill you anyway! Hurry! He'll kill us both! He'll kill us both in front of the kids! He has guns!"

I groped for clothes speed-dressing into Levi's, sweatshirt inside Santa coat, found cowboy boots, no socks. Levi's would not button. Kicked off boots, ripped Sharon's Levi's off me, found and pulled on Santa trousers with my Levi's inside, back into boots running.

Sharon hissed, "Not that way, for God's sake! Out the window! Wait! Wait!" and hands pulled me to one side of the window.

Waiting, peering around the edge of the window, I saw the illuminated interior of a car parked at a facing angle. Both doors on the driver's side were open, throwing two parallel trapezoids of light on the ground. Killer barked and leaped around a shadow moving in the farthest trapezoid and I saw a man leaning through the rear door. The man straightened a sleeping little girl up to sitting in the backseat. He tried to shake her awake. Killer joyously jumped front paws up onto the man's backside and lurched him over into the car. The man, recovering his footing, spun and kicked a yelp out of Killer. With Killer thus tranquilized silent, the man leaned back inside the car and shook the little girl, stroked her hair, tugged her ears.

Sharon hissed in my ear, "They're supposed to be at goddamn Disneyland! For the whole goddamn weekend!"

The little girl stirred. The man leaned over her and lifted an even littler sleeping boy out of the car. The man gave the girl another shake and left her waking up in the car light while he carried the boy into the house. The man was big. I heard him order Killer out of the way, then another yelp.

My fingers joined Sharon's, fumbling the window screen loose. I swung a leg over and out and suddenly remembered, "My duffel!"

Hands shoved me out the window. "Hide! I'll get it!"

As I passed the front of the car the little girl inside opened sleepy eyes and saw me. A yard light came on over the door of the mudroom. The man came out the door and I only had time to duck down on the other side of the car.

Bootsteps approached. I heard a growl, close, and found Killer looking around the back bumper at me. Killer lunged. I bellied into the dirt under the car with Killer barking and snapping after me. I fended with a forearm and he chomped hold of my sleeve. I staccato filliped his nose hard while he held on to me enraged and snarling through clenched teeth. On my other side, snakeskin cowboy boots, size giant triple-wide, stepped into the trapezoid of car light on the dirt in front of my eyes.

A voice that matched the size of the boots said, "Killer, leave the damn cat alone!"

I yanked my arm free, wincing at the loudness of a rip, and scrunched millimeters out of Killer's snapping reach.

"Killer!"

Killer ran around the back of the car to the other side, where pink running shoes descended to the light on the ground, tiny beside the scaled behemoths scuffing dust in my face. I turned my head and gagged for breath, holding the beard over my mouth to keep from gasping out loud. I swear those boots were as big as armadillos. I remember suddenly wondering if snakes that big were poisonous when I felt teeth take hold of my trouser leg. I found myself being dragged slowly, steadily, backward.

Eyes and throat full of dust, I fought to stay where I was, digging fingers, fingertips, fingernails into escaping dirt, grabbing at the gradually passing underside of the car and burning my hand on the muffler.

Killer backed out from under the car with my red-veloured leg locked in his jaws, snarling triumph, just as the car doors closed and the ground alongside went dark. Tiny feet and giant feet became silhouettes against the distant yardlight.

"Son of a bitch!" the man yelled.

I shut my eyes, certain he had seen my leg, expecting huge hands to join Killer's teeth in dragging me out upside down from under the car and for the rest of her life the little girl would never be able to forget the night she saw Daddy killing Santa Claus.

As I lay there facedown at yet another dead end of my life, a solid wallop sent Killer howling away.

"Get in the house, asshole!" the man commanded. Then he groaned and said in a pained voice, "Want me to carry you, baby?"

"No, Daddy," the little girl said yawning. "It's not good for your back."

Voices and silhouetted feet receded with Killer toward the house, tiny feet stumbling with sleepiness.

"Daddy, I saw Santa Claus."

"Not yet, baby. Not till Christmas Eve."

"No, Daddy. Really. I really saw Santa."

The Christmas Kid   81

"Hey, that's good luck, you know. It's real good luck to dream about Santa right before Christmas."

"I wasn't asleep. I opened my eyes and I saw him."

"You're so lucky."

At the door of the house Killer tried to hang back, but the man booted him in with a "Git!" ahead of the little girl.

I lay under the car trying not to make any noise, choking, spitting dirt, burned hand rubbing more of it into blinded eyes, too scared of the yard light to move. My eyes watered and I kept panic-rubbing dirt into them until I calmed down and let them fill. I forced myself not to rub my eyes and they overflowed, then I could open them enough to blink cleansing tears. The door of the mud-room opened and I jumped, cracking my head on the crankshaft.

The house was a stinging blur to me, sideways from under the car. A shape I knew was Sharon appeared in the doorway. Behind her, death in the moving shape of Killer tried to exit around and between her legs. Sharon swung a dark object at Killer and disappeared, chasing him back inside the house. Then the dark object flew out the door and landed in the dirt as my duffel. The door closed. The yardlight flicked off, on, off.

I slithered out from under the car and crouched behind it, waiting for the light to go off in the kitchen. Late night, early morning, I had no way of knowing. I was still feeling the wine. I looked up at the stars in the cottonwood, but they told me nothing.

While I waited for the kitchen to go dark so I could retrieve my duffel and get away, the wine and my exhausted survival-shock got me lost looking up at that tree full of stars and thinking about it as a kind of clock, a clock whose movement of stars I could not read, what my father calls a *"sidereal chronometer,"* at least in winter without the leaves that also made the tree a calendar, a calendar of seasons and a clock of winter stars.

Then I was thinking of Davy. The stars always make me think of Davy because he knew so much about them. One Christmas Dad gave him a big book on astronomy. Davy pulled an old canoe we had out into the snow in the backyard and lay in it nights with the book and a flashlight, bundled up and blanketed against the cold, teaching himself the constellations. I was little then, with an earlier bedtime than Davy, and I watched him from my bedroom window. I could never see Davy lying in that dark canoe in the snow, only the astronomy book intermittently appearing in his flashlight. Every time the flashlight went off and the book disappeared, it meant to me that Davy was looking back up at the stars with something he had just learned about them. When the snow melted, he kept at it. I watched him out in the canoe a couple of moonless nights every month for a year. From my window I tried with binoculars to read the astronomy book by Davy's flashlight, waiting long dark moments for the light to reveal it and then quickly never quite catching a glimpse of what he was studying. All I got out of the project were the colds that Davy kept coming down with—"*astral catarrh*," according to Dad, complicated later that spring by the "*sternutatious pollinosis*" of hay fever. Davy taught himself the names and stories of the stars of the constellations and when, where, and how to find them all by means of each other. He could distinguish the planets by their movement among the stars. Our father, the ardent amateur etymologist and expert on the Old West, did not know, until Davy told him one night at dinner, that the word "planet" comes from Greek and means wanderer. The night sky was a year-round clock and calendar and map and mythological storybook to Davy. Growing up he was always pointing out planets and connecting stars into constellations for me, then for Fred and later for Matt, always giving us bearings we never needed because we were with him. If the stars were all it took, Davy would have out-survived any of Dad's heroic mountain men. Over the years he made me, then Fred, then Matt at least learn to recognize Orion and how to find the North Star, the only light in the sky that never moves, by drawing a line through the two pointer stars opposite the handle of the Big Dipper. Because, Davy said, knowing just that handful of stars will always keep you from losing your sense of direction. You may not know exactly where you are, but your sense of direction will tell you at least where everything else is so you can never be absolutely lost. Fred and I kidded Davy a lot about going down with the Titanic or waking up stranded someplace with nothing but the stars to tell him where everywhere else was while he was sliding down the deck or eating his shoes. Which, Davy always said, was exactly his point: you may be stranded, starving, freezing, treading shark-infested ocean, helpless, hopeless—but even if your few familiar stars cannot save you, they will never fail to give you your bearings. You will know, Davy said, which way is Kansas City and can turn your last breath toward Stroud's. Doomed but never lost, that was Davy.

16

I did not see Sharon's kitchen light go off. When I remembered to look, the whole house was gone in dark. I could not see anything but the cottonwood against the stars and found my duffel by tripping over it, shouldered it, and snuck away as quietly as I could, terrified that at any second the blind silence would explode into Killer at my throat.

The dark closed in even scarier as I felt my way down that switchback through the avocado trees. The trees were black and the passage down through them was a winding blackness, steep dirt twisting through trees so close that the stars were nowhere but directly overhead and it was like going down into a hole—a hole belonging to whatever it was that Sharon and I had heard from the safety of her pickup.

I tripped and fell in invisible ruts, scared to death of odd noises off in the trees. Worse, though, were the sudden leaves in my eyes. They spooked me so bad that when another avocado conked me I stopped and furiously groped leaves for it and, feeling it, tore it off and threw it as hard as I could. I waited to hear it splash down in distant trees, but I must have thrown it straight up because it crashed back through branches at my shoulder and scared the living hell out of me. I panicked.

The adrenaline of panic may be the purest form of human energy, a mindless surge of survival-overload that can enable a ninety-two-pound anorexic, emphysemic, arthritic mother to lift an Oldsmobile off her child.

I admire adrenaline junkies like bullfighters and kamikaze downhill ski racers and white-water canoeists and great world-class cat burglars. Or anybody who seeks and courts and forges their own fear into more or less graceful rituals of life and death. They fascinate me because my own panic is the more typical instantaneous insanity of a human trying to fly. It must be some vestigial or atavistic reflex from all those millions of years we lived and leaped for our lives in trees.

I whirled and the centrifugal force of my duffel, heavy with the textbooks I had intended to sell, yanked me sprawling off the road through avocado branches that grew thick to the ground. Fighting to crawl clear tangled me deeper and I got completely turned around losing the road in eye-whipping, beard-snagging, duffel-seizing blindness. The earpieces holding on the beard fit tight, securely twisting my ears when it snagged. The duffel over my shoulder caught and held me with my arm trapped in the strap.

Terminal claustrophobia set in. I thrashed for escape, and stabbing branches might have poked out my eyes if the beard had not suddenly grabbed unyielding, threatening to wrench off my ears.

The pain persuaded me not to move until my mind could come back with something, anything to help me.

Stillness brought me the familiar slope of the ground. With the fingers of my loose hand searching and finding and freeing the beard, I felt which way branches forked and narrowed. I shifted and backcrawled that way, freeing my duffel, which gave back my arm, and kept crawling backward until first my knees found the ruts of the road and then the blackness emptied of branches and leaves.

Fire drills. Bomb drills. CPR. Your transoceanic 747 becomes a glider at forty thousand feet. In case of emergency, proceed to the nearest procedure. PROCEDURE SAVES LIVES!!! I realized that I needed a *procedure* to get me out of that avocado jungle.

My first procedure was simply to crawl down the braille of the ruts. After tangling with the trees, the slow, unhindered progress of this was calming. Until I sank my unburned hand deep into a warm and stinking pile left quite recently by a large animal I hoped was not carnivorous.

This immediately inspired me to my feet and into my second procedure, which was to center myself in the wandering descent by spreading my arms wide and slowly tacking to keep the creature-filled trees at my fingertips.

Crawling was faster. I tripped down over the ruts back and forth under a drifting glimpse of useless stars, steering by flinching at leaves. Slow and blind as evolution. A dead end of evolution. Body trapped in glacial progress, mind racing volcanic panic. Brain racing to keep steady and stay in my mind. Thinking of *Deliverance* and paddling stroke by stroke downriver. The road could have been a dry riverbed, walled deep and narrow, perfect for a flash flood. A torrential churning avalanche of guacamole. Or warm with the strangling stink of my hand. In case of emergency, proceed. Things could always be worse. How worse? No stars. Useless stars are better than no stars. The stars are forever. Nothing is forever. Dead is forever. Prove it. I will never see my brother again. Not in Stroud's, anyway. Never forever. I will be older than Davy ever was. I will forget. I will die remembering. Every night under Davy's stars. He made them his by knowing about them. Davy told me that the starlight from the Big Dipper takes seventy-five years to reach earth. And that's close compared to most stars scattered even more millions of light-years away. Astronomers can now image the birth of the universe—because stars die, but their light keeps traveling. Every night of the world. Stars over primordial ooze. Stars over dinosaurs. Stars over ice. The beginning of the universe over the end of the world. Silence over silence. Nameless over nameless. Every night of the world over my brother's grave. Leaf-flinch . . . rut-trip. How the fuck did we ever get to the moon? From that first escaping squirt out of the primordial ooze, out of what my father calls *"the old etiological bouillabaisse"*—flight-panic, curiosity, whatever—to men riding fire to the moon? How much had to happen? How long it all had to take? "Ad Astra per Aspera" is the Kansas state motto: "To the Stars Through Difficulties." Adrenaline junkies, astronauts and slam-dunk float artists, runback masters of the blur and vanish, ballet and gymnast and diving magicians of gravity, the conjuring dexterity of really fast short-order cooks and bartenders . . . we worship the *flyers* among us. From ooze to the trees to the moon to the stars. Which makes the Olympics, according to my father, *"our quadrennial planetary ritual celebrating the progressive evolution of the human body."* Faster, farther, better, unlike me. The Olympics and the American presidential election occur together every leap year. Davy taught me that. Davy taught me how to remember how many days there are in each month by counting the months forth and back across the knuckles and spaces of my fist. Davy taught me how to tie my shoes and how to tell time. He taught me that Easter always falls on the first Sunday after the first full moon after the first day of spring. A favorite family legend has it that when I was very young Davy traumatized me with the mystery of the spoon, first showing me his own reflection right-side up on the convex side— bulbous and looking like Jiminy Cricket—then turning the spoon around to show me myself upside down. The family tells me I took the inverse image of concavity as a serious personal failing. They say I cried the house down. Davy calmed me by showing me my convex image right-side up like his, then I turned the spoon around and saw myself upside down again and wailed back into despair. I would not stop crying until Davy showed me that he also was upside down inside the spoon. I tested the phenomenon with my mother's reflection, with my father's reflection, with the reflection of all four of us together in a tiny family portrait to make sure that everyone and not just I was upside down inside the spoon. I grew up taller than Davy. No matter how big I got, though, Davy always knew more. He taught me so many things, often, as we got older, before I had a chance to find them out on my own. I learned to hide books I was reading so that Davy would not talk to me about them and tell me their endings or, worse, spook me with story details or some symbolism I had missed. To this day, obsessive reader that I am, I always wonder what I am missing. There was no such thing as trivia to Davy. Nothing was too small to matter.

He and Dad, between them, seemed to know everything. Growing up I remember always trying to come up with things neither of them knew. Just one little piece of information about some subject they knew everything else about made my day. If I did not have a fact, I peppered them with questions to stay in their conversation.

But not this night. This night the Wizard was in blind solo descent, arms spread groping leaves, Santa Claus escaping down the bean stalk. Honest to God, mister, your wife told me she was divorced! I swear it on my beard! I swear it on all those shoes I should have asked about in your mudroom.

I imagined Sharon with her husband and her kids in a happy family portrait, all together upside down inside the spoon with Killer and the cat and singing "I Saw Mommy Kissing Santa Claus." Once I thought of it the melody kept going through my head and I heard myself singing it as I stumbled down zigzagging the ruts. My voice sounded strange to me so I laughed out loud to buck myself up, a deep big-bellied Santa's *"HO! HO! HO!"* and to my amazement, the gap in the treetops opened full of stars and I walked out onto the paved road at the bottom of the mountain.

17

aved but exhausted, I decided to get some sleep just off the road in an orchard. The rustling night noises spooked me, though, so I climbed branches and secured myself as high as possible among avocados.

I dreamed I was back on the mountain, not descending but scrabbling up the steepening passage. My shadow was dark in front of me. The passage rose sheer to my face, and my shadow reached for my hands as I climbed. Then I was stuck clinging to my shadow, with no way to go and gravity pulling me loose. I started to slide. There was no hold, no way to stop myself so I let go and rode the mountain. I swung around headfirst, sliding on my shadow down the mountain and suddenly I was standing, surfing the biggest wave I was ever on, racing a cavernous tube of white water. The wave steepened into a whitening green blur on which my shadow again stood up beside and just ahead of me. Spreading my arms for balance, my shadow reached back for me and vanished as the white roar overtook and surrounded me. I was in the tube, the Green Room, every surfer's ultragoal, hurtling upright inside the breaking wave.

I have never ridden the tube; even in dreams, before this one, I always wiped out or bailed out as it approached. Here I was inside the holy spinning ice-green gloom, expecting awe but more surprised and horrified by the sickening stench of it. I crouched for speed to escape, to get back out with my shadow, but the tube closed, steadily swallowing me. I wiped out and was sucked under and pounded into a bottomless whirl, drowning, gagging in sewage. Panic woke me to what I suddenly realized was the shit-stink of my hand under my nose. I flinched away from it and fell crashing through branches.

After the wake-up call, I climbed back up to get my duffel. The shifting weight of all the books in it nearly pulled me out of the tree until I just let it drop. Disburdened, I still managed to fall again.

It was still dark and I was shivering. I put on the stocking cap and the beard helped, too. On the road I headed instinctively toward first light. As I walked, the sky ahead lightened and brightened and the darkness around me turned into trees. I could see my breath. I had a terrible headaching hangover thirst from the wine and the smoked saltiness of the ham. But my overriding priority was to find a gas station or any place with hot water and soap. My hand stank so bad I tasted it.

I found a two-lane road that disappeared in both directions into lemon groves. I continued on toward the dawn, passing endless rows of trees. Now and then a farm road intersected, also vanishing into the trees that closed off every distance.

A pinpoint of light appeared way up ahead in the dark under the dawn, growing slowly, coming a long time while it brightened and separated into the headlights of a semi headed for the coast. I stuck out my thumb, intending to get back to Ventura and call Fred for that bus ticket. The semi, straddling the centerline, blasted by me in a windstorm of dirt and rocks.

Walking was warmer than standing still, and I kept on east to watch the dawn seep up the stars. The dark ahead became a ragged silhouette of mountains. The mountains seemed to rise higher as clouds piled up over them, delaying and prolonging the sunrise. My destination was behind me, but the intensifying flux of colors was too beautiful to miss and studying them took my mind off my hangover.

Everything inside my mouth felt unfamiliar. Along with my newly chipped tooth my other teeth did not bite together as usual but were twisted and shifted into strange alignment and crowded by my tongue, which was a roughened ill-fitting shape, dry and swollen to about the size and lolling weight of a lesser iguana. I pulled the beard down to my chin and walked along mouth open to air the awful taste.

I was holding out for oranges but finally gave up and picked a lemon off a tree with my less-offensive burned hand. I chewed through the yellow hard dust and insecticide and lemon bitterness of the peel and spit it out to suck the pulp. The sudden flooding sourness stung, like biting down on an electric shock. My salivaries surged to life in a burning spasm and my whole face contracted in an implosion of puckering. Opening my eyes, I squeezed some of the juice on my stinking hand. The liquid, evaporating, chilling my skin in the cold air, detonated a gagging reek of lemon-scented shit. I vomited.

I walked back onto the pavement holding my toxic hand out dripping away from me at arm's length. Having so enlivened and enhanced transmission of the odor, I tried to deaden its reception by sucking on the lemon while carrying it in my mouth.

The sun came up over the clouds, stabbing my eyes with hangover pain, and I was just about to turn around for Ventura when a horn honked behind me. Tires squealed and I whirled, biting on the lemon, to see a tow truck skidding off the road, fishtailing broadside on the shoulder, banging tow chains and cables and hooks and everything loose in a mushroom cloud of dust right at me. I was dead sure it was Sharon's husband come to kill me. I dove into a lemon tree, belly flopping hard through branches and swimming for my life while flying dirt sprayed the leaves above me.

For a long moment dirt rained down out of the tree and the dust cloud billowed past, slowly revealing the tow truck at rest, headed the opposite direction, five homicidal feet past the spot from where I had jumped.

The driver's side was to me and on it something darker than the background developed out of the dust, accruing detail until I was looking at a huge snake profiled head down, yellow eye glaring and fangs gaping in fierce mid-strike. I thought it was some kind of weird logo painted on the side of the tow truck. But then I saw three-dimensional live human fingers emerging from the two-dimensional snake's wide mouth and realized that the resolving apparition was tattooed from hand to shoulder of a bare arm gripping the outside of the driver's door. The good news was that it was not Sharon's armadillo-booted husband who owned the arm and who sat at the wheel looking wildly around for a run-over Santa Claus.

The driver's door opened and the wearer of the snake hit the ground running, searching all around the truck. He was shirtless, pale, skinny; I saw more tattoos.

"No, Lord! *Please!*" he yelled, dropping to his knees in the dirt. Pleading hands lifted and aimed the snake at the sky.

"Please! Please! Please, Lord!"

He closed his eyes and summoned courage with a deep breath, held it; then the snake went down and his ass went up as he looked for my body under his truck. Not finding me, snake fangs rose back to heaven as he reclasped his hands and reclosed his eyes and his breath exploded in thankful shouting.

"Thank you, Lord! Again, Lord! As always, Lord!"

Crisis passed, he lurched to his feet and I saw that he was beatified by more than gratitude. He reached inside the truck and brought out a tequila bottle that was mostly empty.

"Santa!" the tattooed man yelled at my lemon grove. He drank from the tequila bottle. "Hey, Santa!"

I stayed hiding.

"*SANTA CLAUS!* I am *SORRY!* Need a lift, Santa?" He saluted, hitting himself hard in the head. "Yessir, Santa! All the way! You and me, Santa!"

He stood still, listening.

"*WHERE TO, SANTA!*"

He took another swig.

"SANTA!"

He drank again, turned, and smacked his forehead hard against the truck. He dropped the bottle. His shoulders shook. I thought he was choking until I heard him crying.

"Santa, please. It's me. Rudy. Rudy. All her life my mama's favorite son." He hit his head on the truck again. "Oh, Mama . . . Mama . . . Mama." He sobbed, hitting his head on the truck every time he said it. "Please, Santa. Not you, too, Santa. Santa . . . Santa . . . Santa." He pounded his head on the truck and his sobs deepened into helpless moans.

I couldn't stand it. I got to my feet and walked out of the lemon grove. Coming up behind him I started to put a hand on his heaving bare shoulders, but they were covered with tattos I didn't want to touch.

"Hey," I said.

He turned and, seeing me, made no attempt to stop crying or to wipe away his tears.

"She did it, Santa. She did it to me. At Christmastime. Santa, she hates me."

"She doesn't hate you."

"She threw me out."

"She still loves you."

"She don't."

"Your mother always loves you."

"Not Mama. The cunt!"

"Don't talk that way about your mother, Rudy."

"The cunt did it!"

"She's still your mother and she loves you."

"No—"

"She does."

"No—"

"Yes, she does."

"Mama loves me!"

"You know she does."

"Mama loves me! *THE CUNT DON'T!*"

"Who's the cunt?"

"Wife's the cunt! The cunt that did it!"

"You sober up and go home."

"No more home. Just you and me. Santa and Rudy. Faithful Rudy."

"Sleep it off, Rudy, and go home. Your wife's worried about you."

"She can kiss old Flutterbutt."

"Beg pardon?" I should not have asked.

Rudy grinned through his tears at my question and turned and, before I realized what was happening, he dropped his pants to show me the wings of a giant butterfly tattooed in many-colored kaleidoscopic detail and convex symmetry completely covering his buttocks.

"Pretty, huh?" Rudy asked back over his shoulder. "What you call a conversation piece."

I was speechless.

"A real icebreaker with the ladies, if you know what I mean." He winked, turning and pulling up his pants. "Now, where to, Santa?"

"Thanks anyway, Rudy."

"Come on. Where you headed?"

"No, Rudy."

"You headed home? Where's home?"

"Home is Kansas City."

"Kansas City it is! Nonstop! Delivery to your door! Santa!" He flung an arm out at the tow truck and nearly fell over after it. "Your sleigh is waiting!"

I shook my head. He was so drunk it was like saying no to death.

"Hey." Rudy squinted one eye shut to speak conspiratorially, also perhaps to keep from seeing double. "We don't have to go to Kansas City if you don't want. We can go anywhere. Anywhere you say. We got highways, Santa. We got my wrecker. At your disposal. Any folks in car trouble along our way, we'll come to their aid. Santa and Rudy. They'll never forget us."

"You're a drunk driver, Rudy. A public menace. With luck, you'll only kill yourself. But that truck is such a tank, you'll probably just walk away sorry about your victims."

"Well, hell . . . if that's how you feel . . . you drive!"

18

I *drove. East. The* tow truck was big and boaty, hard riding, rattling and wandering all over the road. I kept overcorrecting back and forth over the centerline, compounding Rudy's already swaying impairment so that he couldn't find his mouth with his tequila bottle.

"Kick her up to seventy," he said, "and she'll steer herself."

I was in motion, setting the claustrophobic green valley in motion around me, behind me. The endless rows of trees right and left spun by like wheelspokes and the centerline ticked in under the left front fender, weaving less as I got the feel of the wheels confidently over the speed limit. The clouds ahead had broken up into a string of cumulus, blue-shadowed white in the sun, flat-bottomed all exactly at the same altitude and billowing up the thermals on the desert side of the mountains.

I suddenly had it made clear to Kansas City. Flagstaff by dark, Santa Fe by morning, then up the entire Santa Fe Trail and home by tomorrow night. No need for bus fare. No disappointing Fred. Easy.

My only problem now was my right hand stinking up the confined inside of the truck. Even Rudy, drunk as he was, wrinkled his nose at the increasing stench and we both rolled down our windows without a word.

"So, Rudy?" I asked, trying to take his mind off his nose. "What's with the wife? What's the trouble there?"

Rudy reached around to show me the list of names tattooed on his scrawny white noodle of a right arm. All but the last two names on the list were crossed out by tattooed Xs. They were all names of women, maybe a dozen.

"Came home last night with this," Rudy said tapping the newest name on the list, freshly darker blue in the center of raging inflammation.

"Wendy," I read.

"Wife's name is Edith."

Edith was the last name on the list above Wendy, the only other name not Xed out.

"Who's Wendy?" I asked.

"I have not a clue."

"You don't remember?"

"Not a goddamn thing. But here she is on the honor roll. Had to be a goddess. Nothin' but a goddamn goddess makes the honor roll."

"That's quite a blackout."

"I miss a lot of shit."

"You black out all the time?"

"Don't have to lie about what you can't remember."

"What's the worst place you ever woke up in, Rudy?"

"Don't want to talk about it."

"What's the best then? Rudy, what's the best place you ever woke up in?"

"The best?"

"Where was the best place you ever woke up and found yourself?"

"The best I ever found myself . . . ?" Rudy pondered, enjoying the question. "The best?"

I waited.

At last Rudy grinned at his answering memory and said, "Puppies."

"Puppies?"

"Woke up once with a litter of puppies sleeping all over me. Old mama mutt growling at the cops. Threatening to protect me like I's one of her own."

"Don't your blackouts scare you, though?"

"Shit hell, no. How else you find a goddess? How you think I found my Edith? Come to one day and there she is next to me in the sack. Both of us hungover and beat-up like we're shipwrecked together. Like the Lord give her to me in my sleep and ever since then she's this dream I can't wake up from. Washed up with her like Adam and Eve. Rudy and Edith. My Edith is a goddess. Goddamn goddess cunt!"

"Coming home tattooed with another woman's name is pretty serious, Rudy."

"Edith knows serious. She knows it had to be a goddess. Goddesses hate each other's guts. Cunt!" Rudy twisted his arm up and licked the new tattoo. "Wendy!"

"Too bad you don't remember her. I mean, to get yourself such a load of trouble—"

"Was worth it!"

"How do you know?"

"This tells me." He kept licking the inflamed name on his arm.

"Tells you what? Here you are paying for something you don't even remember. You don't know what or even if it really happened. All you've got is the trouble."

Rudy licked his arm and, lasciviously smacking his lips, said, "I got Wendy."

"Wendy's just a tattoo."

"Listen, Santa. In the blackout of this our earthly veil, a tattoo makes all the difference. You ask yourself. What's for life? Outside the Lord and amputation, what's yours and stays yours for life? Your mama don't. Cunt don't. People change. You change. Shit hell, you don't look at a mirror every day in five, ten years you won't even know yourself. It goes. You go. Santa Claus goes."

"Santa Claus goes to Kansas City, Rudy," I thought to myself.

"Goes gone. With the Easter Bunny and the Tooth Fairy and your mama and your own goddamn face in the mirror. Everything changes and you forget it like it never was. Lose it like you never had it. Like there's no fuckin' difference. No fuckin' difference between forgetting it and never having it. But a tattoo makes the difference. A tattoo beats all that forgetting. I do not, cannot, shalt not remember Wendy. But *this* . . ." Rudy slapped his arm and winced at the soreness. "*This* tells me I did time with a goddess. Tells me I was fuckin' there, Santa, and I come back alive. Fuckin' there and fuckin' here!"

"Herpes and AIDS are forever like that," I suggested.

"That's what I'm saying: *Forever!* A tattoo is fuckin' forever! Hey, and when you die you take it fuckin' with you. You and me, Wendy!"

"What about Edith?"

"Edith's got her own tattoos."

The stink of my hand did not go away with the windows down. Noticing it again undiminished, Rudy shot me a suspicious look and jerked his feet up one at a time to see if he had stepped in something. He sniffed under both his arms. I kept innocent conscientious eyes on the road, now winding up out of the valley, while Rudy fidgeted and squirmed searching first himself, then the cab around him for the source of the excruciating smell.

I was double-clutching a downshift into a climbing curve when Rudy leaned over to check the floor under the dash. He recoiled from a sudden close whiff of my hand and plunged his head vomiting out the window. *"Laughing at the wind,"* my father called it whenever I got carsick. I shifted up, accelerating out of the curve as smoothly as I could while Rudy hung there. After a moment he slumped back inside, wiping his mouth and leeward cheek with a shaking hand, took one reviving breath, and lunged vomiting again out the window.

I began to fear for my miraculous nonstop deliverance home, afraid an ailing and sober Rudy would start wanting his Edith. While I was worrying, Rudy opened his door at seventy miles an hour.

"Gonna sack out," he said, hauling himself out into the wind. He swung a tequila-heavy leg around and clambered after it until all I saw of him was a hand gripping inside the door frame. Watching Rudy instead of the road, I lurched into a curve too fast and his hand disappeared as the truck skidded sideways whipping the door open, and I corrected violently slamming it shut. When I could look back, horrified certain that Rudy was bouncing down a mountainside, I saw him in the truck bed sprawled resting on his back with a tattooed arm over his eyes.

I pulled over, got out, and gave Rudy my duffel for a pillow. He opened bleary eyes, surprised and grateful like a sick little kid as I folded it under his head for him. I put the tequila bottle in his hand for insurance. There wasn't much tequila left, but I wanted to get every mile I could out of it.

19

*O**ver the top** of the valley I caught freeway and made good time down through the mountains. The Mojave opened out below, immense flatness, sunny but strewn with huge shadows of scattered clouds. I waited until the Palmdale turnoff to stop, leaving Rudy asleep while I got myself and the Santa Claus suit cleaned up in a men's room at a gas station. Twenty miles later, in Pearblossom, I stopped at a liquor store and shoplifted a fifth of tequila, with which I hoped to keep Rudy headed east.

The Pearblossom Highway, California 138, becomes California 18 straight east along the desert side of the San Gabriel Mountains until I-15 shunts you north across nothing to Barstow, where I-40 is your last interstate chance not to go to Las Vegas.

I watched the mountains recede, dwindling in the side-view mirrors, twin postcards of snow crests sinking into the desert. The tourist hype is true: you really can leave the coastal sunshine of L.A. and be skiing the San Gabriels in an hour, climbing on your way to a view of the city clear to Catalina Island twenty-six miles out in the Pacific when you can see it through the smog. You can ski and surf in the Christmas heat wave, all in the same day.

Unless it's raining, even the weather always seems to be on vacation in L.A. People arrive from everywhere, take off their clothes, and commence to reinvent themselves starting with the tan. L.A., where waiters and salesmen and car mechanics and real estate agents and carpenters and delivery gigolos and guys who clean swimming pools and even the hookers on the Sunset Strip are probably only supporting their acting habit and everyone including your dermatologist is meanwhile collaborating on a screenplay. *STAR-WARTS*. Coming soon. Waiting to hear.

The desert got chilly at eighty miles an hour, but Rudy stayed dead to the world. I drove in and out of bright sun and those long gloomy cloud shadows with the heater up full blast and both windows down, warm with my stocking cap and Santa beard whipping in what was for me merely fresh air, nearly to Barstow, before I heard pounding on the window behind my head.

Red eyes looked away from me weeping in the wind. The rest of the face looming in the rearview was blue, gaunt sunken cheeks blue with cold and beard stubble, varicose nose and shivering lips as blue as his tattoos. The wind whipped his shaggy hair like flames through split-second various ways to comb it. The speeding transformations were hypnotic. His face was a tragic mask ruined senseless with cold and alcoholic aftermath, but his hair raced animated through wildly exuberant other Rudys, each escaping into the next. I couldn't take my eyes off it in the rearview as I pulled over, slowing across the right lane and Rudy's hair time-lapsed, writhing, subsiding into a tangled helmet as we came to a stop on the shoulder of the interstate.

Rolling with painful care, stiff and slow off the far side of the truck, Rudy suddenly fell out of my sight. I pushed the passenger door open and he reappeared, crawling up inside. He started to say something but stopped short at the sight of Santa Claus behind the wheel of his tow truck. Then he wouldn't look at me. Finally in the seat, he fell halfway out again reaching to close the door. Both of his shaking hands could hardly crank up the window. I rolled up my window and drove on.

The heater had the closed cab stifling in seconds. I took off the stocking cap and beard, but Rudy huddled shivering in the heat, wrapping his stringy arms across his bony concave chest and rubbing the tattoos on his shoulders and arms for warmth that would not come. Grimacing at the sight of the desert, he closed his eyes and shook his head at waking yet again in hungover ignorance of where he was.

"Where the hell is this?" Rudy asked, eyes closed.

"I-15. Coming up on Barstow."

Rudy sighed and shook his head again keeping his eyes closed. "How far's Oxnard?"

"Hundred fifty miles or so."

"Drive."

"Rudy?"

Rudy sighed again, still keeping his eyes closed. Goose bumps stippled the snake on his arm.

"Rudy?"

Each of Rudy's goose bumps was an individual hair follicle rising over its own tiny deepening shadow. The snake seemed to be stirring to life with them, blue scales ruffling, and I nearly jumped out of my skin as Rudy exploded into furiously slapping and pinching his cold shoulders and chest and arms and yelling, "Drive! Drive!"

"Rudy, we're headed east!"

Rudy stopped beating himself and opened his eyes at me. "East?" He looked at the interstate vanishing ahead into the desert under clouds. "Where the hell east?"

Kansas City suddenly seemed so far, too far away to mention, so I said, "Edith threw you out last night."

"Edith throws me out every night. One of these mornings . . ." I jumped again as Rudy violently re-attacked himself. "Can't get warm!" he yelled and slapped himself in the face with both hands several times.

I opened the new bottle of tequila for him. Rudy two-handed it for a shuddering taste and got his door open just in time to retch out into the wind. I pulled over as Rudy drank again and heaved again hanging out the door. The wind off the desert combed and recombed his hair while he drank and heaved, drank and heaved.

I got out of the truck to wait while Rudy continued his search for the first drink of the day that would stay down. The wind was cold. Standing in the open driver's door, I could feel the warmth inside the truck. The heat that had been smothering now felt pleasant, inviting. I wanted to be back inside, back in motion; but first I had to let the tequila reprime Rudy for his return trip home to Oxnard via Kansas City. My hope was to head back west with him until he blacked out for a nice long winter's U-turn.

I looked in my duffel for something Rudy could wear. Down under my books I dug out an old forgotten T-shirt.

"Hey," I said through the driver's door to his bowing back. He ignored me. I tossed the shirt in at him and he looked around, one red weeping eye over his tattooed shoulder. "Shirt," I said, pointing where it lay behind him on the seat with my stocking cap and beard.

Holding the tequila bottle in one hand, Rudy groped his way into the shirt, so huge on him that it made him seem even smaller. He got it on backward and did not put his arms through the sleeves so he was just a bodiless barfing head, holding a tequila bottle out the neck of the shirt.

A Mercedes passed honking at my Santa suit and I waved back to two Medusas in hair curlers, headed for Vegas. Or so I assumed from the sequined clothes hanging in the backseat. Most of the traffic, though, was going south toward L.A.

I got my Walkman out of my duffel to have it with me driving, to listen at least to its radio when Rudy passed out again. Expecting only the radio, I was glad to find a Jimmy Buffett tape left in the cassette player. I rewound it and put on the earphones to test the batteries. "Margaritaville" came on clear and strong, cheerfully drowning out Rudy's retching while I waited on the shoulder behind the truck.

The wind gusted hard, cold out of the east. Nothing but desert stretched away east and west on both sides of the interstate. A deep shadow passed over and, humming along with JB's tropical anthem, I watched the desert brighten as the sun came out from behind a cloud. The shadow swept away west, going fast across the interstate.

The sky was full of clouds now scattering shadows everywhere over the desert, big gray-bottomed white clouds and their deep blue shadows all drifting west. The shadows traveled faster across the land than the clouds floated in the sky. It was still morning and the low winter angle of the sun lengthened the shadows and threw them well ahead of their corresponding clouds.

"Margaritaville" played and I got involved matching individual clouds with their shadows as they crossed the interstate. The project evolved into betting myself that a certain distant shadow would converge on the interstate with an approaching northbound car. It was going to be close and I was mentally cheering both shadow to catch and car to escape when, feeling dirt and gravel spraying up my backside, I turned, hearing only the music, and saw the tow truck peeling out.

I chased, screaming at Rudy with "Margaritaville" in my ears, but the tow truck accelerated away. I saw brake lights and dust and started running again as it stopped in the distance. The brake lights went off and Rudy got out. He dragged my duffel off the truck and lobbed it into the desert. I stopped running. Rudy got back in the truck and tore off in a high-speed illegal U-turn across the median, in the bucking course of which he threw my Santa beard and stocking cap out his window.

I gave him the finger as he blasted south past me. Rudy waved the tequila bottle and I caught a last glimpse of the snake on his arm rising out of my shirt.

I watched the tow truck disappear, not noticing when "Margaritaville" ended or anything else until the next song started and I turned it off and pulled off the earphones and marched up the interstate mad as hell to find my duffel, landmarking it somewhere off the road in the distance roughly opposite where my beard lay visible on the median, a white speck between double lanes of highway surrounded by desert.

20

It was less than twenty miles to Barstow where I-40 starts east. A twenty-minute drive, most of which I walked in the next three hours. It was too cold to stand in the wind and wait for cars. I didn't listen to my Walkman because I wanted to be able to hear cars coming behind me. Drivers honked, none stopped.

The sun went in and out of the clouds, their shadows sweeping over me as I walked and walked that endless vanishing highway through cactus all around to the horizon. The horizon was as flat as the sea. The clouds gathered out of the east and I watched their shadows merging west. I passed the trudging time distinguishing varieties of cactus, all motionless, monuments of evolutionary success in the buffeting wind.

The sun went behind one cloud for a long time and I could see sunshine way out in the desert all around me, the western edge of the light racing away, the much farther eastern edge of it coming slowly. When the cloud passed the sun brought out my shadow beside me on the interstate. Turning with my arm up high to raise my thumb to approaching cars, my shadow reached across both lanes. I watched cars drive over my shadow walking backward.

I was hungry again. Trying not to think about it, or about the cold and the weather closing in, or about Rudy and the ride I had deservedly lost, I imagined how things could be worse.

Worse would be walking the interstate at night when the winter cold would be lethal; or in the midday heat of summer; or at night in summer when the rattlesnakes crawl out of the ocean of cactus to warm their cold blood on the human pavement. Walking a twenty-mile ribbon of rattlesnakes at night between hurtling Vegas-bound traffic on my left and black snake-filled desert on my right definitely satisfied my search for worse. With a mind like mine, who needs drugs?

Though I come from landlocked Kansas, I try to think like a sailor—always expecting worse—so I am often terrified but seldom surprised by my chronic disasters. My drowning nightmare in the avocado tree was not unusual; it recurs in one form or another all the time and I wake up swimming in sweat, tasting my own salt in the dark.

But as familiar with worsening disaster as I was, waking and sleeping, I was amazed at how dangerous being Santa Claus had been so far. Everyone the suit had brought me into contact with was somehow out of control: Heather and Randy high on forbidden college-killing hormones and apprehended together at police gunpoint sixty miles from home; Sharon; Killer, who tried to eat me; Rudy, covered like a men's room wall with tattooed grafitti and stoking himself mindless with tequila.

As usual, I had to put myself at the instigating head of the proceedings. But where were the family station wagons bound for Grandma's house with Dad at the wheel and Mom dispensing sandwiches to backseats full of singing children and good sound Labrador retrievers? Where were the four-wheel drives, the off-road landcrunchers crammed with ferociously healthy skiers munching trail mix while they described past gung ho runs and wipeouts with the gestures of fighter pilots? Where was the Porsche with the lovely heiress?

It was the week before Christmas and Sharon, mother of two, had worn my beard while she undressed both of us. She wore it through everything we did in bed—in my whirling blindness the beard accompanied the featherstrokes of what I did not realize at first were her breasts tracing my face and finding the rest of me, and I felt the beard wherever she put her mouth on me—all of which did not seem so perverted at the time, in the context of the unpronounceable wine and the dark, as it did in daylight walking across the desert.

At first I tried to blame the Santa Claus suit, rationalizing that behind the wheel of every vehicle was a potential Sharon or Rudy or some other, even more vengeful thumbsucker out to get even with Santa Claus for being a childhood lie. When Scrooge was not aiming down at Christmas shoppers from his bleak suicidal sniper's ledge, he was probably cruising the highways of our republic, making up his own obscene lyrics to "Jingle Bells" and "O Come All Ye Faithful," and stalking some needy Santa Claus to hit-and-run.

Deep down, though, I knew it was not really the suit's fault. It was the Wizard, not Santa, who had conned Heather and Randy too far from home. It was the Wizard, not Santa, who had participated, no questions asked, in mutual seduction with the bearded mommy. It was the Wizard, not Santa, who had schemed alcoholic enslavement of Rudolph the Tattooed Retard. Santa Claus had only got them to stop their cars. The Wizard did the rest.

21

Watching my shadow fade in and out with the fleeting sun became a project, counting my steps while my shadow was gone to pace off and time relative cloud sizes. Finally a cloud took my shadow and I gave up counting when I looked up and found the sky solid gloom. The whole desert was dark with a last few scraps of sun blowing away west.

Then the wind backed around out of the north and intensified, a slamming cold headwind against which I pulled the beard up over my nose and the stocking cap down over my ears. The wind still stung my eyes, so I was walking backward in it, a faceless bandit Santa, when I thumbed a car that surprised me by stopping after it passed.

Squinting into the wind, I saw skis racked on the roof, California plates, and an Oklahoma Sooners decal across the bottom of the rear window. A young teenage boy in the backseat and a woman passenger up front were both spinning their heads watching me and arguing with the man at the wheel.

All three fell silent as I opened a back door and got in with the kid, who shoved over as far from me as he could get and still be in the car. It was a big comfortable sedan—lots of legroom even with my duffel and three pairs of ski boots on the floor under my knees—and most important of all, it was warm.

"Thank you very, very much for stopping," I said in my best and brightest, most courteous frozen college boy's voice, the voice that rings with a mother's pride and her eternal maternal gratitude for any stranger's kindness to her son. "It certainly is a pleasure to get out of that wind."

"I'll bet," the man said as we retook to the road. His voice was not as angry as the way he stomped the car up to speed.

"Yes, sir," I said recovering from the whiplash that coldly infuriated the woman in front of me.

I seemed to be a problem, but I did not care. The acceleration sank me back in the seat and weariness made it voluptuous to be off my feet and riding warm. I was suddenly so tired and sincerely thankful.

"I really can't thank you folks enough," I heard myself say.

The woman faced forward, silent, refusing to acknowledge me. The man looked over at her and she refused to acknowledge him as well. I looked over at the kid and found him staring at me. My smile elicited no response from him.

"Where you headed, Santa?" the man asked, breaking the silence but not the tension in the car.

"Kansas City, sir. Trying to get home from college for Christmas with my family."

The Sooners decal told me they might be good for a long ride all the way into Oklahoma. This must have been the case because the woman, hearing me say Kansas City, traded a look over her shoulder with the kid, her son I assumed from the resemblance. Then they both turned hostile eyes on the man, the woman beside him silently but openly threatening, the kid behind him, who looked nothing like him, shaking his head in safely unseen teenage disgust. I had my work cut out for me.

"Kansas City's not so far," the man said after a long moment and immediately changed the subject. "What college do you go to?"

"Caltech. I had a plane ticket home, but it was one of those airline deals where it's only good for a certain flight on a certain day and I missed the darn thing."

From the back I saw the right side of the man's grin as he said, "Christmas parties."

"No, sir."

"Just screwed up, huh?"

"No, sir."

The man winked at me in the rearview and said, "Was she worth it?"

Hearing this, the woman traded another look back with the kid. The kid shook his head at her and sighed. The woman faced forward. The man was hopeless.

"It wasn't a girl, sir."

"Oh." Hopeless.

"No, yes. Yes, she was a girl," I said improvising, "come to think of it."

Hopeless winked again, just between us men in the rearview.

I went on. "Her name is Marilyn."

"Marilyn," he repeated, drawing out the syllables, savoring the name on his lips and in his mouth.

I went on. "Marilyn Monroe."

"Marilyn Monroe? At Caltech?"

"Yes, sir."

"Marilyn Monroe at Caltech." The man laughed, looking over to share it with the woman, who was not amused and refused again to acknowledge him. He retreated to the rearview and asked me, "Does she live up to her namesake?"

The woman's hands rose in exasperation with a portable headset radio, an old one with an antenna and big earphones that she carefully brought down around her blonded bouffant.

"Sir," I said, "my Marilyn eclipses her namesake." The kid was staring at me again so I grinned and winked at him and added, "Totally."

The kid's Neanderthal lack of response made me suddenly realize that I still had the beard on up over my nose. I pulled it off, but the correction made no difference to him.

"Gorgeous, huh?" The man could not get over it. "And at Caltech."

"The most grogeous little white rat you ever saw."

"She's a rat?"

"Part of an experiment I'm running at school. Sorry, sir, for my little joke."

The man really liked this.

"Marilyn Monroe is a rat!" he said and laughed to the woman, who paid him no mind as she gazed out at the desert, oblivious in her headset. He shifted in his seat to share it in the rearview with the kid. "Marilyn Monroe is a rat!"

The kid looked out at his side of the desert. The man quit laughing alone.

I went on. "Things got critical early in the morning I was supposed to leave for home."

"Marilyn OK?" the man asked.

"Well, sir, let's just say that, thanks to Marilyn, we're about to make a major, major breakthrough."

"What in?"

"Are you at all conversant, sir, with cellular genetics?"

I have learned the hard way, over and over, to make sure I am not engaging some expert in his or her own field. I once offered fictitious karate tips to a beautiful and sadistic stranger who did not tell me she was a Black Belt. Another time I hustled myself into high-stakes video game competition with a brushcut nerd who turned out to be a Navy pilot headed for astronaut training. It is deadly to get caught playing the other person's game.

"I'm a rag man," the man said.

"Beg pardon?"

"I'm in the clothing trade."

"Well, it's difficult to explain, sir. But putting it in layman's terms, very simplistically, we're about to settle the environment-versus-heredity question as it relates to survivability."

"Survivability?"

I could not help myself, it was like singing. "Within a statistical population. By measuring individual personality adaptability to a constant flux of physical and, therefore, psychological stress."

The kid was staring at me again. Over the headset in front of me the antenna wagged to music that only the woman could hear.

The man asked, "But how do you measure something like that?"

"Qualitative and quantitative analysis of neurological response." I winked at the kid, Mr. Wizard confirming, "Computers."

"What isn't?" the man said.

"I devised a program that enables us literally to read Marilyn's mind, analogizing her thought processes while she made her way through a maze of IQ-measuring difficulties."

"Analogizing?"

"Translating into computer code. Like recording."

"So when you play it back . . . you've got a computer thinking like a rat?"

"A genius rat. Exactly, sir. And the computer enables us to extrapolate from analysis into synthesis."

"Say what?"

"We take her thought processes apart and put the smartest stuff back together."

"Just like the rag biz. Knocking off your high end."

"Thanks to Marilyn, our next step is to program her already superior and now vastly computer-enhanced intelligence into individuals of average IQ, all of whom got lost on their own in the maze, and then we'll measure their performance improvement."

"With Marilyn's intelligence in their brains."

"With Marilyn's intelligence *idealized*. Showing them through the maze. Exactly. Leaving out any flaws of her learning mistakes. Looking for the slightest improvement in any statistically average individual."

"Kind of like Marilyn's a ghost."

"A perfected ghost. Exactly, sir."

"Perfected into a guardian angel or something."

"Exactly."

The man shifted in his seat to say to the kid in the rearview, "The lights are on and nobody's home, but *GOOD NEWS: THE HOUSE IS HAUNTED!* Just what you need."

The kid, irritated by what was apparently a family sore point, reached inside his shirt collar and lifted elegantly miniaturized, state-of-the-art earphones from around his neck to his ears. He put his head back and closed his eyes and, wrapping deft fingers around a cassette machine I now saw on the seat between his legs, he emulated his mother into oblivious privacy.

The man looked from the kid to me in the rearview and asked, "Which is it?"

"Which is what, sir?"

"You know, survivability. Is it heredity or environment?"

"It seems to come down to the fundamental difference between what you're born with and what you learn."

"Heredity is what you're born with."

"And environment is what you learn. But if heredity doesn't know enough to learn from environment, then, you see, life gets lost in the maze."

"With all those average rats," the man said with a look at the kid in the rearview.

"Exactly."

"But who needs heredity when you've got Marilyn Monroe?"

"Exactly. That is exactly what my experiment is aimed at finding out. How does heredity relate and adjust to environment? How does environment call forth and shape the resources of heredity? How does environment *become* heredity? Those average rats, you know, never even learn they're in a maze, much less ever find their way through it. The stress puts them in a daze and they try to hole up and weather it out."

I kept this conversation going, working like hell to wangle myself into a long ride. The woman's antenna subsided into a motionless tilt and I could hear her snoring while Hopeless, Jr., manipulated his machine without opening his eyes. The man needed company.

In Barstow we stopped for gas and the man got out to check the tires. The kid opened his eyes and ignored me. The woman's antenna remained at her sleeping angle. I had to go to the men's room, badly, but knowing how unwelcome I was in the car I did not dare leave it.

The kid got out and wandered off to the men's room, stuffing his cassette machine into a front pocket of his jeans, leaving me alone with the woman. My bladder had me squirming, knocking my knees and curling my toes, and the family's next stop was probably not until Arizona.

I looked over the seat at the woman. She looked as though she had died in her headset. Her mouth had dropped open and her chin was lost in the accordion folds of her neck. The man was busy under the hood now, checking the oil while the attendant sloshed and squeegied the windows clean. The kid reappeared inside the station pretending to poke around the curios while browsing girlie magazines, still wearing his earphones wired into his pants. Desperate, I opened the car door and snuck slowly and as quietly as possible out of the car and dashed for the men's room.

None of the family saw me go, the car was still getting gas, the hood was up, the dipstick was out, and I hurried. I mean, I *moved* it, crippled graceless under pressure in a bladder-bursting burning frenzy to get back to the car. During which I heard tires squealing away, and when I ran back outside, the car was gone. My duffel was waiting for me on the ground.

"Man said to give you this," the attendant called, tossing the white beard to me.

The beard had been folded and rolled and something fell out of it as I caught it. I picked up wadded paper and smoothed out a ten-dollar bill.

22

I **took the rag** man's ten-dollar bill down the main drag of Barstow, California—old Route 66, famous and dead—to the golden arches of a McDonald's. Inside McDonald's was festooned with Christmas decorations and warm with its standardized mouthwatering smell. I was the only customer at the counter, behind which three high school girls in uniforms and paper elf hats giggled at my Santa suit and pushed each other to avoid being the one to take my order. I carried my laden tray to a window table, giggles bursting behind me as the girls regrouped.

My duffel in the chair opposite, white beard tossed atop it, stocking cap atop beard, made a pudgy slouched companion. Besides us the place was empty except for a strange guy wearing yellow aviator glasses who kept watching me while he stayed glued to his mobile phone, grinning at me as I built and ate my ritual Quarter Pounder (ordered with extra lettuce and tomatoes so they have to customize it fresh off the fire) with cheese, extra pickles, one packet each of ketchup and special sauce and two packets of pepper, two large orders of fries also elaborately prepared each with three packets of ketchup and four packets of pepper, and two cartons of lowfat milk.

The guy bothered me with his grin. His clothes were expensive casual chic, dark slick. Everything about him was dark with the elegant sheen of an evil prince. The evil came from his eyebrows; behind those yellow glasses, his eyebrows grew together in a solid black arc over amused eyes that would not look away from me. When I got up and came back to my table with cherry pie, apple pie, and coffee, he was sitting in the seat beside my duffel.

I sat down across from him and kept my mouth shut, determined to outcool him into speaking first. He sat smiling at me, at ease and unembarrassed in his own waiting silence, watching while I stirred the last of my milk and three packets of sugar into my coffee and waited for my pies to lose their inedible heat.

I did not wait long enough. When the first bite of cherry pie instantly burned away any cool I had, he snapped his fingers and shook his head in disappointment. With a move like a magician's, his other hand appeared with a roll of bills. He pulled off a twenty and tossed it on the table between us.

"I was wrong," he said.

"Wrobowha?" I said around the pain frying my mouth.

"I was betting you'd save the cherry and eat the apple first."

My tongue stung like it did when I was nine years old and a nun scoured my mouth with soap. I am not a Catholic, but little blond Ann Coughlin was. She played the cello between her lanky knees and ever since the second grade I would have followed her into hell, which is exactly where I found myself that one time I went to her Sunday school and made the mistake of debating with Sister Torquemada.

The evil prince's hand appeared again with a business card, which he placed on top of the twenty. He slid the twenty with the card on it across the table to me among my desserts. The card read, *"George Talarian, Public Relations,"* nothing else but a phone number with a toll-free 800 area code.

"Where is this?

"Everywhere," George Talarian said through his grin. Some dentist had earned a fortune on his caps; they were perfectly straight, flawless white oversized models, with enough reflective candlepower for George to read open-mouthed by moonlight or conduct rheostatic seduction. I think of George Talarian wearing dark glasses to shave, tanning himself with his own smile in the mirror. He pointed out the window at the only car in the parking lot, a black Corvette with Nevada plates. Black-tinted windows made the car a solid gleaming capsule. "My office. You on the road?"

"How about a ride to Kansas City?" I joked.

"How about a ride to Las Vegas?"

"It's out of my way," I said, mentally drooling to ride in the black speed machine. *To Vegas!* "Or I'd love to."

"Vegas is on the way to anywhere."

"I'm headed east," I said, "and I have to get there."

"East goes out of Vegas, doesn't it?"

It began to feel like the conversation I am always having with myself, rationalizing pros and cons of some potential disaster, gambling with worse, setting myself up for yet another brilliant recov-

126 *Michael Allin*

ery. I looked out the window again at the Corvette and tried to change the subject.

"You've got a hell of an office."

"And you've got a hell of a scam, kid. *Santa Claus on the Road.* But a scam is only as good as where it works. Works best. Hey, Edison didn't know what to do with his lightbulb until electricity told him."

"Why Vegas?"

"Dead time. Every year, this godforsaken week before Christmas. Town's like a farting corpse. New Year's? Jackpot. Christmas?" He closed his eyes and stuck out his tongue to describe Christmas in Las Vegas with a weak and pathetic raspberry, his rendition of a flatulent corpse. Then he opened his eyes and said, "I could make you into an event."

"What do you mean, 'An event?' "

"Vegas is dead, Santa. And you're alive. You're *high concept.*"

" *'High concept'?*"

"Like the word 'mother'—everybody's got one. Or at least, and more important, an idea of one. *'The Hitchhiking Santa Claus'* is all you need to say. This one week of the year, for one night— tonight—I could grease The Hitchhiking Santa Claus into a major Vegas happening."

"For openers?"

"For openers I get one of the hotels to put you up humanitarian gratis for the night."

" 'Room at the inn.' "

"The night of your life, by the way, Santa."

"I find that definitely *high concept.*"

"Jackpot. Which gets you coverage rippling out across the

whole country. Dream jackpot." George Talarian grinned. He sat back in his chair and put his arm around my duffel, stocking-capped and bearded in the chair beside him. "And tomorrow morning you wake up so famous you ride it all the way to Chicago."

"Kansas City."

"You want KC, fine," he said, idly combing his fingers through the beard atop my duffel. "You ought to want Chicago, where your exposure can expand open-ended. Talk shows. *People* magazine. KC can't take you national." As he spoke his fingers found and kept toying with the little white pom-pom on the end of the top of the stocking cap. "A great idea is limited only by what you want it to do for you."

"I want it to get me home to Kansas City."

"So ride it through Vegas," George offered, opening both hands without letting go of the pom-pom between his thumb and forefinger. "Have that night of your life in a comp suite at let's say Caesars. Get yourself some tit-for-tat publicity to speed you on your way. And see what happens. All on the house."

"How about a plane ticket from Vegas to KC?"

"No promises. But hey"—he opened his hands again still holding the pom-pom—"anything's possible. Believe me, Santa. You're standing under lightning with this."

Certain, if I held out, that I could score a plane ticket home from Las Vegas, I said, "Thanks, all the same. But it's out of my way."

"Believe me," George implored, laughing, promising, "Vegas will get you home! Home with the world at your feet!"

I looked out that window of McDonald's, telling myself to hang tough, to forget the Corvette and the night I could have in Las Vegas instead of on a bus to Kansas City, to stand pat and put it all on the plane ticket home. Looking from the Corvette across Route 66, beyond the windy strip of roadside business and the train tracks that follow the legendary highway, I saw nothing but desert and gray sky.

"Out of my way," I pretended to think out loud to myself. "And I'd lose the rest of today and all of tonight for traveling."

George said nothing. I looked out the window. I felt him watching me, waiting for me. I let him wait. Finally I turned and looked straight into his grin.

"Get you home jackpot," he whispered.

"Jackpot is a plane ticket."

"Believe me."

"I'd need a plane ticket."

"Under lightning. With the world at your feet."

"I'd love to help you out. Be fun."

"Help yourself, Santa."

"I'd have to have a plane ticket."

George shrugged. I shrugged. George sighed and stood up, his arm inadvertently knocking the stocking cap and the beard off my duffel. He retrieved them from under the table and dropped them in the chair where he had been sitting. We shook hands and he headed for the door. I had my familiar sinking feeling.

"Thanks, anyway," I called after him.

"Every deal begins with a no."

"Merry Christmas."

"Humbug!" George laughed, leaving, shouting back to me across empty McDonald's. "Thank hell it's almost here and gone!"

He waved and flashed his grin at the three elf-hatted girls behind the counter who all waved back smiling sweetly until he was out the door and they all looked at each other and giggled.

We all watched George get into the Corvette. The sound of a Corvette firing up always gives me goose bumps. George reversed, giving us a beautiful sweeping look at the car from back to front, then circled the parking lot the wrong way, slow and rumbling past the window to wave at me. The big engine shook the ground. Even inside McDonald's I felt it through the floor and up through my seat and my coffee trembled in the cup on the table. George's black window rose and he disappeared inside its reflection as the Corvette pulled out onto 66.

Without the stocking cap and beard, my duffel now looked like nothing but a duffel. It was getting late in the day. The weather was closing in with the early winter dark. And I had blown the night in Vegas. The night of my life.

"Shit," I yelled at myself, evoking shocked giggles behind the counter.

I still had George Talarian's card, though. I also had his twenty dollars. Not only had I eaten for free, I had made money on the meal. The Wizard was ahead of the game, I told myself, looking out the window. The afternoon was already darkening the restaurant windows into mirrors. I stood up and put on the stocking cap.

"Shit," I said to my reflection, whispering this time.

On my way out I stopped at the counter and ordered three apple pies to go, but the girl told me that all they had was cherry.

"Are you like hitchhiking?" one of the girls who was not helping me asked.

"Are you going to L.A.?" the girl who was helping me asked.

"Vegas, I bet," the other girl who was not helping me said. She was a little older than the other two.

I shook my head at all three and said, "Kansas City."

"Oh, my God!" all three responded in amazed unison, identically with that rising teenage inflection, exactly as Heather had said it to me cruising down the coast in her mother's comfortable leather-scented convertible way back it seemed so long ago. The phosphorus flashed in the waves. Was it really only the night before? The night of Sharon and her avocados and Killer? With the nervous energy of hunger now gone, I was dragging tired, feeling low.

" 'Oh, my God,' " I quoted, agreeing. "Can you direct me to the Greyhound station?"

Two of the girls directed me down the main drag. The girl with the bag containing my cherry pies handed it over the counter to me. I held out money to pay her, but she waved it away.

"Good luck," she said.

I was so surprised that all I could say was a lame "Gee, thanks. Thanks a lot."

"Merry Christmas," she said.

"Yeah, Merry Christmas. Thanks. Really."

In my tiredness, surprised, not knowing what else to say, I headed for the door.

"Merry Christmas!" the other two yelled and the older girl who bet I was headed for Las Vegas added, "Keep your thumb warm, Santa!"

Behind me the glass door closed on their giggles. Walking away across the empty parking lot, I looked back and we all waved through the window.

23

The next Greyhound to Kansas City was three hours away, and I had time to kill before Fred got home and I could call her to credit-card the ticket. The station was just a small storefront and I waited inside while it got dark, reading *Deliverance*, until the guy in charge told me he was shorthanded that night and had to lock up while he went home for dinner.

"Three hours to hurry up and wait," the guy said as he walked away down the sidewalk.

The cold wind had dropped, so instead of going back to wait in McDonald's, I strolled the bright lights of downtown Barstow, a short stretch of mostly motels and gas stations. Across 66, into which every street in Barstow dead-ends, a slow freight train clattered east, car after car after car with both ends out of sight, longer than the whole town. I felt the new souvenir chip in my tooth with my tongue and kept walking.

One of the smaller mom-and-pop motels was decorated with

Christmas lights, strings of blinking colors along the roof and around the door of the manager's office. More lights outlined the vacancy sign, which bore the message *"Strangers are just friends we haven't met yet."* The lights flashed their different colors one at a time at scattered random, a bright and cheerful holiday welcome, homier than the big chain motels with all their advertising neon.

Between the twinkling motel and the curb, a floodlit plastic snowman stood beside a picnic table in a patch of dead lawn. The snowman wore a battered top hat, an authentic, once jet black silk stovepipe now ruined into jauntiness, tilted to one caved-in side, its top ripped and standing open like the lid of a tin can. A plastic carrot-nose supported giant sunglasses with frames two feet wide. The eyes of the snowman were big lightbulbs, one yellow, one white, each blinking independently, so close together that the snowman was crosseyed behind the huge dark lenses.

I dropped my duffle on the ground and sat down at the picnic table with *Deliverance*. The winking eyes of the snowman were bright enough to read by, but first I got involved watching the Christmas lights on the motel, studying them for any pattern or predictable rhythm to their blinking. I thought I had discovered a relationship between a green and a red over the door of the manager's office when I noticed a face in the window, a woman, watching me. I waved to her. The woman did not wave back. She kept watching me. I opened *Deliverance* and read for a while, and when I looked up again the woman was gone.

I tried to wink along with the loony snowman, coding the long and short flashes of his yellow eye, then his white eye, as the dots and dashes of Morse, deciphering in each a different unintelligible but endlessly repeated message. Then I suddenly remembered another snowman, a real one from a long time ago.

Back home there used to a security cop at Country Club Plaza who always hassled me and other kids about riding our skateboards through the mall. He wore a mustache, so, of course, we called him Adolf Rent-a-Cop and saluted him with the Nazi "Sieg Heil!" as we zoomed around, baiting him to chase one of us. We were a nuisance, and he was our dependable local bully. Provoking and escaping his charge made you a man among boys. One winter day Adolf resorted to ambush; I wiped out and he confiscated my board. My father had to go retrieve it. Adolf Rent-a-Cop's version of my legend, together with the arm I had broken wiping out and the concussion that had me seeing colors in front of and around everything, caused my father also to confiscate the board. A few nights later it snowed and the next morning there was a six-foot snowman in the fountain with the statue of Pomona at the Plaza. The snowman was wearing Adolf Rent-a-Cop's hat, somehow stolen, under which the head was faceless except for a piece of black comb broken to the shape of Hitler's mustache. The snowman had mannequin arms, hands wearing black gloves also stolen from Adolf, one raised in Nazi salute, the other fondling a breast of the statue of Pomona, Roman goddess of vineyards and orchards. Someone tipped the newspapers in time for them to get pictures. Reports made no explicit comment on the similarity between Adolf and the snowman, but the afternoon editions ran photos of both wearing the hat. One action shot showed Pomona wearing the hat with Adolph up in the fountain holding on to her while he kicked down his effigy. Suspicion fell on me. My alibi, however, was air-

134   *Michael Allin*

tight; fractured humerus, at home cozy and out of it with my concussion. My mother had kept waking me up to check if my eyes were crossed. It snowed again that afternoon and through the night. The next morning there were half a dozen more snowmen scattered around the plaza, all faceless look-alikes with broken-comb mustaches and Nazi-saluting arms. The snow stayed on the ground for over a week and Hitler snowmen appeared in the plaza every morning, despite stakeouts and the offer of a reward, amount undisclosed, by Adolf himself. Davy and Fred were seniors in high school then, and on every one of those mornings Davy made it a ritual for the three of us to be at the plaza before dawn. Friends of his from the football team and other interested citizens would meet us and the group of us would follow Adolf around the plaza, cheering him as he took a baseball bat to snowman after snowman. It would have been easier for him simply to strip each snowman of its offending mustache, but the situation drove him crazy. Davy made sure it drove him crazy, organizing it so Adolf became more and more angrily and impotently convinced that I was the punk kid masterminding his humiliation. Adolf found me waiting for him every morning with my nightly whereabouts accounted for and a beautiful older redhead, Fred, on my broken arm, in the protective company of my big brother and his even bigger friends and several unimpeachable adults, one of whom was a cub reporter for the *Kansas City Star* who stayed with the story until the snow melted. It was not until after Davy died that Fred revealed to me that she and Davy had built the first snowman to avenge my broken arm. Fred had stolen Adolf's hat, with his gloves in it, off a coatrack in a café in the mall where he was having coffee. She and

Davy were more amazed than anyone by the subsequent continued appearance of so many other snowmen. Other people had it in for Adolf, or maybe it was college kids with a new rage. Whoever it was, I learned probably everything I know about revenge, and a lot more about being brothers and how dangerous a family can be, watching Adolf Rent-a-Cop murder snowmen on those frozen mornings in the witnessing company of Davy and Fred and our group of regulars. Some of us brought thermoses and extra cups, cups of hot coffee and tea and cocoa steaming in our hands in the cold. You could see everyone's breath. Fred and I pretended I was a gangster; she was my moll and our breath was cigar smoke. I was ten years old and everyone signed my cast.

I could not see my breath there in Barstow, but it was cold with the wind picking up again. I put on the stocking cap and beard, and sat with my back to the road to avoid attracting attention from passing traffic so I could concentrate on *Deliverance*.

Pages later, oblivious on the river in the story, I heard a strangling hiss coming from the ground under my duffel. I looked down, wondering what the hell, as another hiss rose between my feet under the table. Suddenly remembering the rattlesnakes I had imagined on the highway, I whirled at yet another hiss behind me and caught a blast of needles in my eyes. Blinded, I grabbed my duffel and received an uppercut from under it before I escaped into the street.

Wiping my eyes revealed sprinklers sputtering and coughing out of the sorry little dog patch around the snowman. Long dormant, overgrown, and clogged, each sprinkler spouted its own ragged and pathetic variation, no two alike. The one between my feet splattered up against the underside of the picnic table. The one that had given me the uppercut, released from under my duffel, geysered straight up seven feet in the air.

The woman from the motel had come outside to turn the water on me and was now retreating to the open door of the office. The wind blew the sprinklers at me.

"Merry Christmas!" I yelled into the spray, leaving to get out of it. "Merry fucking Christmas!"

The woman stood in the doorway, framed by the blinking Christmas lights. When I was already leaving she bravely waved me on my way with her sprinkler handle.

I was wet. My duffel was wet. *Deliverance* was wet. My beard was dripping. I yanked it off walking and the wind blew the water I shook out of it into my face.

"NO PRESENTS FOR YOU!!!" I yelled back at no one. The woman was gone, the door was closed. The wind whipped the sprinklers into a wild flying blizzard around the snowman, so dense that he disappeared and all I saw was the blizzard glowing yellow or white with the flashes of his eyes.

It was colder being wet in the wind. My duffel was heavier wet. I stowed the book and the beard and stocking cap, all soggy in the soggy green canvas. I took out my Walkman and put on the earphones to make sure the machine was all right, then turned it off to save the batteries and stuffed it inside my Santa coat. I kept the earphones on; they were better than nothing against the wind.

Too cold to stand still, I was walking nowhere fast, marching shivering deaf to anything but the rattle of my teeth, when I felt the ground rumble.

The black Corvette crept alongside me and I slowed my marching speed. The car slowed with me. I stopped. The Corvette stopped, gleaming all over with the reflected neon colors of the Holiday Inn behind me. I saw my own reflection hunching cold and windblown, looking like hell in the tinted passenger window, vanishing as the window lowered to reveal the grin of George Talarian.

24

I *did not have* to go to Las Vegas.

After that skateboard wipeout when I was ten, my parents were more worried about my concussion than about my broken arm. I am not pleading consequent lifetime brain damage, merely explaining why I do not remember the rest of that day. Two things at dinner that night stand out, though.

One is my knocking over a full glass of milk with my new cast and everybody yelling while I just sit and watch the whiteness spreading at me toward the edge of the table. I am mesmerized by all the concussion-colors flashing in the advancing whiteness until Davy tosses his napkin on it and stops it from cascading into my lap. Napkin, milk, and cast are all the same white flashing colors and I am very, very happy to see that my cast has this in common with Davy's napkin. I was really out of it.

The other thing I remember at the dinner table that night is my father trying to explain to me his theory that there are basically two types of people in the world: *matches* and *candles*. *Matches* are those people who, according to my father, ignite things and make things happen; *candles* are those who illuminate and keep things going.

"Best to be both," I remember concluding.

"Best is not my point."

"What's your point, Dad?"

"My point is that each needs the other."

"Right. If you're a match, then you can light your own candle," I said, ten years old with a fractured humerus and a concussion. I still believe this to be the unarguable ideal.

"What if you're a match without a candle?" my father asks me. "Or a candle without a match?"

"Yeah, that's what I mean," I answer, concussed.

My father laughs. "What do you mean, that's what you mean?"

"I mean, that's my point, Dad."

"It's not *your* point. It's *my* point."

"Well, we agree."

"We do not agree. You say it's best to be both. A match *and* a candle."

"Right."

"I say you can't be both".

"Oh. Then I disagree."

"A candle can't light itself. A candle needs a match. And a match is no good—no lasting good, anyway—without a candle. A match needs a candle to harness its—"

Lost in my father's analogizing, I interrupt with practicality, "Which are you, Dad?"

"I'm a candle man. Insurance is illumination. Like a lawyer or a doctor or Fred's dad stockbrokering or any professional taking care of people's problems."

"Which is Davy?"

"Davy is a match. A self-starter. Definitely. Matches like Davy ignite the fire and candles like me harness it into light. Heat and light, see?"

"Which am I, Dad? If I can't be both. A match like Davy or a candle like you?"

"You?" My father laughs again and knocks his knuckles on my cast before he says, "You're a moth."

I did not have to go to Las Vegas. I could have called Fred and caught that bus to Kansas City. And even if I had missed the bus, I had George Talarian's twenty dollars in my pocket. Twenty was enough to get me off the road for the night in a cheap motel. Enough to sleep warm and clean.

But not this moth.

25

*I*t had taken me twenty-four hours—a long night of life, threatening wear and tear, and most of a cold day walking upwind across the Mojave Desert—to make that 150 miles from Santa Barbara to Barstow. The next 150 miles to Las Vegas took about ninety minutes.

George kept the Corvette at 110 mph, immune to cops by virtue of a radar detector. A gift, he said, from friends at the Las Vegas Police Department. He gave me a pair of night-vision binoculars and assigned me the skywatch, which meant glassing the clouds ahead for highway air patrol. At 110, George did not worry about patrol planes coming up behind him.

"Between fifty-five and a hundred," he said, "opens their window of opportunity on your careless speeder."

With his radar detector, light-gathering binoculars, yellow-tinted aviator glasses, his double shoulder-harness racing-model seatbelt, black kid driving gloves and matching Brazilian handmade driving moccasins, George Talarian was a serious speeder. We could not have traveled that fast for that long carelessly.

On a long straight northbound stretch of empty highway, George centered on the broken line dividing the lanes and stopped to demonstrate Corvette acceleration from a standing start. Revving, gunning rpm's like a man infuriating a lion, George popped the clutch and first gear was like being fed to the lion, zero to thirty-five in three screaming seconds. The digital speedometer then blurred through the speed limit before George punched into third. I wiped away tears and we were in fourth. George took me to 150, where the only thing I remember is that the broken line under us became a solid white streak. After the demonstration, 110 was comfortable.

The radar detector alerted well in advance a few times and George slamslowed to legal. From 110 the Corvette could decelerate to a full stop in five seconds, to 55 in a fibrillated heartbeat.

My father loves to quote Isaac Newton's description of his debt to prior scientists—*"If I have seen further it is because I have stood on the shoulders of giants"*—and whenever he repeats it the next thing he always says is that Einstein stood on Newton's shoulders to discover the mathematics that incorporated Special Relativity into General Relativity, which led other scientists to formulate the physics to blow up the planet and/or escape to other stars.

"Like cheerleaders," I bait my father, "climbing into a human pyramid."

Newton, no doubt, would be grateful to Einstein, and proud of his own contribution to potential human pyramidal immortality; but I bet he would have killed for a Corvette. *"A body in motion wants to stay in motion!"* And the faster the motion, the more a body wants to stay that way. Whenever George slowed and we crawled past cops at half our velocitized momentum, I physically craved to be rocketing back up in triple digits. The speed was addictive.

Most of the cops we passed were hiding around curves or roadcuts or overpass abutments. We passed a sign shaped and painted to look like the side of a cop car with a real cop car hiding behind it. Another cop car was parked behind a sign advertising the next of a chain of curio shops—*SOUVENIRS GIFTS IDEAS*—twenty miles up the road. A couple of times the detector betrayed radar but the cops remained invisible. There were no patrol planes. Maybe George was right about outrunning them. Maybe with that wind blowing all day on the desert and the weather threatening, the cops were not flying.

We flew. Under the wind so low to the ground that the narrow dark of the cockpit felt as though we were whizzing along inside a shadow. The Corvette was a wonder of aerodynamics, a raked shark-shape skimming even lower and more stable, tighter to the road, deeper in the shadow, the faster it went. Wind speed pushed it down with a palpable sensation of flattening into a blur.

I calmed my inertial panic to hang on by constantly fine-tuning the controls of my six-way power-adjust leather bucket seat, closing the side bolsters more snugly around my shoulders, experimenting with the three separately inflatable lumbar supports, intimately elaborating my comfort and steadying my nerves with a learning procedure that also took my mind off the fact that George drove at such tremendous speed with only one hand on the wheel.

George drove almost the whole trip with one hand because he never got off his mobile phone, wheeling and dealing at 110 to coordinate the increasingly public convergence of Las Vegas with the Hitchhiking Santa Claus. He hustled TV, radio, newspaper, and freelance photographic coverage, with which he then fomented bidding between hotels for the opportunity to accommodate me and participate in my publicity.

The bidding came down to a suite and all expenses, "humanitarian gratis," at either Caesars Palace or the MGM-Grand. George covered the phone waiting for me to decide.

"Whichever'll throw in a plane ticket."

"Go with Caesars," George said, deciding for me. "I can use the gratitude." Then back on the phone, "Tell Wanda she's got herself a Santa Claus. Lemme talk to her."

"A plane ticket," I said while he waited on hold.

"Getting you out of Vegas is tomorrow's problem," he said. "Tonight we are very busy working very hard to get you *into* Vegas on very short notice. And doing very, very well. Stoking the jackpot, baby!"

"Kansas City, George."

"We are riding lightning, Santa!" Suddenly back on the phone as he said this, George's adrenaline-elation did not miss a beat, "Lightning, Wanda! Want some?"

George Talarian was on a first-name basis with every person he called, and he carried every one of their telephone numbers in his head. I have to admit he was impressive on the phone. If the other person turned down George's initial proposition, George proposed it again from another angle, again and again if necessary until it adapted and evolved into a deal or at least made him some points for the future. He reciprocated every refusal with another offer, another suggestion, another question, faceting every difficult sell into a search for something, anything mutually benficial. George was good news calling, determined to share the jackpot with which he was hurtling through the night toward his friends on the other end of the line.

The sky and the desert blacked out around us to nothing but the road in the headlights. I remember having a weird thought that it got darker and darker the faster the Corvette went, that we would slow down into brightening daylight.

George did not take off his yellow glasses, claiming they improved his night vision. When he looked over at me, the lenses reflected twin clusters of dashboard lights. Otherwise, he was a faceless voice in the dark, charming, cajoling, convincing, selling the Hitchhiking Santa Claus into such a wonderful-sounding idea that I forgot he was talking about me. Listening to him on the phone was an education in persuasive intercourse. George did not always get exactly what he wanted, but he always got something.

"Every deal begins with a no." And he ended every conversation laughing with the other person.

26

till on the phone at triple-digit speed, George left-handed the Corvette through a veering climb, smooth but terrifying, into mountains that were invisible in the starless dark. Swooping down the other side we crossed the state line. The blind night was now Nevada.

Far ahead, I saw a faint glow. As we approached, the glow brightened and became cloud cover. There were more mountains that we could see now silhouetted against the clouds, more long tire-hissing curves that rolled the mountaintops rising around us back and forth and kept me refining my seat position against centrifugal panic.

George knew the road so well that, descending a certain curve into blackness, he shouldered the phone to his ear mid-conversation and snapped the fingers of his consequently free right hand for my attention, then performed a slow papal cross from top to bottom and from his side to my side of the windshield—vertical down from heaven to hell and horizontal across the world. Precisely at the end of the last half, the horizontal worldly half of this gesture, the mountains opened and Las Vegas gleamed below us in the distance.

The mountains immediately closed and rose against the clouds as we plunged through curves. George got off the phone and drove for the first time with both hands on the wheel. The bad news was that then he took the curves even faster. At the worst moment of yet another hissing white-knuckler he let go of the wheel again, snapped his fingers, and repeated his conjuring benediction. The dark again revealed Las Vegas disappearing.

"There you are," George said, completing his cross this time with a flourish of twirling fingers in front of me.

I joked him back with a cross of my own against his driving, blessing myself fast because, unlike George, I was hanging on with two hands piloting my seat controls. My *morituri kamikaze* farewell to myself did not insult or embarrass or slow George down at all. Instead it earned me further fright when, in addition to his right hand off the wheel, he took his eyes off the road to laugh at me. After that, aware of my fear, he amused himself by watching me as he executed his big slo-mo cross in every curve.

At that speed every curve was a dropping Deadman's Curve. The mountains opened for longer glimpses of Vegas and I stayed busy with my seat, working like an astronaut in meteoric reentry.

"Lights are pretty, huh?" George said, yawning. Yawning! "Down there in all that dark."

Locked on the lights, I heard myself say, " 'Lost Wages,' " quoting what my father always calls the town.

"Tonight it's all yours, Santa," he said.

"Santa Claus meets the Mafia," I said.

"The mob may have built the town," George said, "but what you're seeing right now from up here—nothing but all those lights—all that electricity comes courtesy of the Indians."

"I never heard of the Hoover Indians."

"Not the dam. The water. The Colorado River flows through the Navajo Indian Reservation. So the tribe gets paid for the water the dam uses to generate the electricity that renders Las Vegas as you now see it—*nightless!*"

"No shit," I said, hanging on against a curve.

"Exactly. Old Navajo saying: '*Man who lives farthest upstream gets paid not to shit in river.*' Which is how come Vegas never sleeps or goes thirsty. Not to mention what the water means to Southern Califoreigners or Aridzona or the whole Western States Power Grid. Look down there at all those lights."

George waved a hand at the lights as the Corvette swung me around another curve, edging a steep drop on my side. I looked and the curve kept tightening, pushing my forehead against the window while the hiss of the tires rose through squealing.

"What do you see?" George asked. He answered himself, "Like looking down on a pot of gold, isn't it?"

"End of the rainbow," I agreed, eyes closed, referring to our arc off the mountain at 110-plus mph.

George did not hear me clearly over the tires and he yelled, "What?"

"Yeah!" I agreed, with anything.

We were sliding, loose in the limbo of a shrieking four-wheel drift.

"What!"

"POT OF GOLD!" I bellowed against the glass, begging for my life and suddenly remembering how they pinned me to the wall for the Mexican who wanted to cut off my ear. When was that? How many screwups, how many passing drivers' faces, how many begged-for lives ago? "END OF THE RAINBOW! YEAH!"

"Amen, Santa!" George whooped, reveling in Corvette chaos control. "We're riding a goddamn rainbow!"

Ride 'em, I begged to myself; ride 'em, Santa; and yelled, "YEAH! YEAH! AMEN!"

We slid, George laughing and whooping to the tires. I opened my eyes to keep from seeing the Mexican with the switchblade, to take my chances sweating it out where I was. At any instant I expected the tirescreaming dark to go silent around one of George's maniacal howls as we floated off the mountain.

He shouted laughing something I could not make out.

"AMEN!" I yelled back at whatever it was he said.

The tires at last subsided into traction. The squashing whirl let go of me. My forehead came unstuck from the glass with a smack. The lights were ahead of us, sweeping across the windshield and disappearing as the mountain flung us into an opposite curve. George let out another yip and affectionately pounded the steering wheel.

"All rainbows lead to Vegas, Santa!" he said.

I got my head back against the seat and kept it there while our tacking dive continued. The mountains on George's side deepened over us; my side dropped into dark. The universal pot of Navajo–Mafia–Santa Claus gold swung back and forth expanding below us, scattered lights now spreading out around the brighter rising runway slash of the Strip; all of it a blur when left turns broadsided so I saw it through the oily smudge my forehead had made on the window beside me. There were no stars. Clouds glowed a low woolen ceiling over the town. Surrounding sky and desert were black. The pot of gold floated up to us like a space station, flattening into a long strand of lights under the clouds as the Corvette mercifully leveled out on the desert floor. Curves kept coming, but they quit dropping. Mere horizontal speed terror was a relief.

The plan was for the publicity people from Caesars Palace to pick me up outside of town. George and I arrived first at the rendezvous, a crossroad overpass where I got out of the Corvette with my duffel in the dark. George was going on to attend to details while I waited for my official ride into hoopla celebrity.

"Practice your 'Ho, ho, ho,' Santa," George said. "Hey, and don't take any rides from any goddamn strangers! No matter what she looks like!"

George gunned the engine in neutral, mounting rpm's in quick earstabbing bursts, and popped the clutch. The rear tires spun, shrieking and smoking, going nowhere while the smoke swirled up red in the taillights and strangled me with the sulphur stink of burning rubber. The Corvette slued weightless in the smoke, then catapulted out of it, accelerating sideways. A speedshift whipped the rear end fishtailing straight and the Corvette wailed off through the gears, taillights dwindling, disappearing toward Vegas before I remembered to breathe.

The sulphurous smoke cleared, but I could still smell it from the cooling tire tracks that started where I was standing and led off farther than I could see into the dark. I could hear the Corvette going a long way after it was out of sight. It faded to a tiny whine, high in the silence between the few passing cars, fainter and fainter until I held my breath to listen to it die.

27

I *waited for the* people from Caesars Palace to come and get me at the bottom of a cloverleaf that looped down off the crossroad into the highway. The highway was still divided four-lane with hardly any traffic either way. The crossroad, swallowed by the dark at both ends of the overpass, had no traffic at all.

The wind was much colder in Nevada, a polar north wind blowing straight down on Las Vegas. I put the white beard over my nose up to my eyes and pulled the stocking cap down over my ears and waited, hoping each long approach of southbound headlights would be my ride. I ignored passing honkers headed for Vegas, so as not to cause one to stop for me. Most of the time, though, there were no headlights coming and no taillights receding up or down the highway and the only sound was the wind.

After surviving the Corvette, it felt strange to be standing motionless and terrorless in the night silence of the desert—velocitization letdown; safe on my feet, but sad, like being homesick.

Swaying from the Corvette and remembering how the train had lulled me to sleep and then had nearly killed me, I started to worry about what worse trouble I was risking with this detour to Vegas. If I scored a plane ticket out of it, I could be home the next day. Say the day after, latest, if I settled for bus fare. I did not want to call Fred. And hitching would be dangerous with the weather turning serious, not to mention the Santa wackos at large on the holiday highways. I did not know how bad the coming storm would be, but the freezing north wind and the heavy clouds over the distant city and the whole black starless sky told me going to Vegas that night was another gamble I could not afford to lose.

In Vegas the Wizard could make a truly spectacular brilliant recovery and I would be home free—moth *through* the flame—with no one the wiser and nothing I needed to apologize for or explain. I was showing up as Santa Claus, of course, as a surprise for Matt. And en route, among the lights strung across the darkness ahead, Caesars Palace awaited me with a complimentary suite and a night I could add to my legend.

Meanwhile, I was headed the wrong way home and going nowhere cold in the desert dark, stuck studying how pinpoints of light drifted loose of the far-off city and grew dividing into headlights that became passing cars that became receding taillights. White lights into red lights, out of silence into silence. One direction passeth and another cometh, but the silence abideth forever. I waited. I shivered. I worried. Evolution rolled on without me while triumph glittered on the northern horizon and failure gaped as big and hopeless as the surrounding night.

Things could be worse, I told myself.

How? I asked myself. What could be worse than this self-inflicted risk, looming with the clouds, warning in the wind, of perhaps having to make my way twelve hundred miles home in a major winter storm?

Calling home for help, I answered myself. Calling home, even secretly to Fred, meant admitting that my life was out of hand, certainly that it was out of my hands. It meant losing every argument, past and future, and raised all future odds against me. It meant forfeiting my own version of myself to my father's opinion.

If I did not score in Vegas, my choices were reduced to index finger or thumb—call home or hitchhike, eat crow or risk the weather. Either way, without Vegas, I was doomed. My brilliant recovery would be just another dead end. Like the Incas, who built a highway twenty-three hundred miles long through their Andean empire, the distance from LA to Detroit, without ever discovering the wheel. History rolled on without them and the conquistadores rolled over them. Maybe in a former life I was an Inca who froze to death trekking the Andes trying to get home and I was still journeying, headed now into my next cryogenic reincarnation.

My worrying, as usual, turned into remembering Davy. I missed him, but it was more complicated than that. I loved him and I missed him loving me. No one will ever know me the way Davy did, and I missed being the person he knew. That person, that part of me had died with him and I didn't know who I was anymore.

Growing up, I was always listening in over my head at the dinner table, interrupting constantly. Conversations between Davy and the old man usually turned into Davy explaining what they were talking about to me. I remember learning that way from Davy how the moon causes the tides and how the earth tilts on its axis as it orbits the sun—the saltshaker Davy made in junior high woodshop circling Mom's crystal sugar bowl—to cause the seasons and bring around their identifying stars. Davy would designate each member of the family as one of the four seasons around the table and plot the celestial calendar with our respective constellations. He taught me that the constellations rise and set four minutes earlier every night, which adds up to two hours earlier every month and brings them back around full circle of the clock every year. This is why the constellations always arrive same place, same time so you can know precisely where their stars will be at each of the 525,600 minutes of the year (527,040 in a leap year) even in their seasons of invisibility during daylight.

"So the universe will always tell you where you are," Davy said. *"It HAS to!"*

Davy was always trying to show me the calendar-clock-navigational map of the earth that the night sky was to him. The only thing I remember is where Orion the Hunter is on both our birthdays. On Davy's, January 31, Orion appears already overhead at dusk, high in the southeast, the three stars of his belt pointing up to the bull attacking him and down to his dog coming up over the horizon behind him. On my birthday 145 days later in the first week of summer, Orion rises and sets 9 hours, 40 minutes earlier, invisible during his entire passage between morning and night in the longest daylight of the year. I do not remember any of my visible birthday constellations because none was as beautiful or heroic to me as Davy's Orion. Davy assured me, though, that if I had special nonexistent dark glasses to black out the sunlight, I could see Orion up there with his dog battling the bull on my birthday, too.

28

That highway to Vegas was so damn dark and cold. To warm up and quit worrying myself sad about Davy, I paced back and forth past my duffel, upwind, downwind, waiting. I got my Walkman out and listened to Jimmy Buffett. I got a cherry pie out and ate it pacing to the music, turning to lift the beard downwind for every bite.

Tromping chomping in cadence and spinning backward into the wind to lift the beard became dancing and pretty soon I was rocking out, Santa Claus berserk beside the highway, trying to fire up some body heat, singing along under the beard at the top of my lungs, then seeing how many different ways I could hurdle my duffel.

I slalomed and karated, pirouetted and kangarooed, limped, stomped, staggered, spun away, and my duffel was a charging bull, a ski jump, a chasm, a fire. I combusted and tried to be flames flailing each move into another, disappearing and unrepeatable.

Then I was smoke wisping, rising, writhing into a ghost, my own ghost, departing. The music brought me slamming back, Baryshnikov battling Bruce Lee, Santa Claus attacking the air, defending against the wind.

I was midair when the ground under me suddenly blazed alight in split-second flashes like staccato lightning, direct hits glaring out the asphalt and my duffel, whiting out everything under me except a frozen strobing glimpse of my shadow spread-eagled, grotesquely elongated and unattached to me.

I crash-landed hard in the dark and went reeling from the white-out into a blackout where I kept on falling, feeling and at the same time watching myself plummet tumbling smaller and smaller. I had this desperate but faraway thought that I had fallen into my shadow, that lightning had struck me or I had died of fright and my shadow was now a bottomless drop. Then my shadow stopped dropping and the asphalt was sizzling my hands as it hardened under me.

I was alive again, still far away but back in the world, slowly coming back burning hands first, blinded by a searing afterimage of the flashes—a retinal overload of colors exploding into colors in the long and jeté-splayed shape of my shadow.

To be blinded by this image of myself seemed the strangest thing yet. My wipeout had knocked me loony. I knew I was on the ground, but it was baffling to be on the ground while seeing myself aloft. Wherever I turned, the outstretched figure hovered before me teeming and seething with fireworks, and I could not understand how it could keep bursting so violently and continuously without exploding its shape. Trying to blink it away only flared it into brighter and more intensely surging spectral flux. And in my looniness, my mind would not let go of the idea that there was something I had to figure out about that spectacular afterimage of my shadow. It reminded me of something I got lost trying to remember. It was something crucial and everything seemed to depend on remembering it, on searching back for whatever it was that was the key to my confusion.

But it was a blank, and the next I knew seizing hands yanked me away from passing headlights, revealing, to my dazed amazement, that I was on my feet. For an instant I thought it was Davy saving me as he always used to, and in the same instant I knew it was not Davy.

The hands pulled me into a group of dark figures clustered around my duffel, upon which I sat down, cherishing its familiarity. Legs surrounded me, faces leaned close moving their lips, talking to me without voices. I looked at my palms and found them strawberried bloody, stinging, it dawned on me, simply from the impact of my crash-landing on the asphalt. Hands pulled the beard away from my face. My deafness became a ceasing blare of music as other hands pulled off my earphones.

29

hey were George Talarian's people, very much under the command of a lady who introduced herself as *"The PR Person from Caesars,"* Wanda. Wanda was an ex-showgirl, flashy blond and weathered by too much desert tanning, but still a knockout with beautiful long legs and a bosom so prominent, even in her coat, that she couldn't see her feet.

Wanda introduced me to her Oriental photographer from Caesars; to a beer-bellied Las Vegas newspaper reporter and his equally beer-bellied photographer; to a pert young local-TV reporter and her silent older cameraman; to a local radio personality who wore a toupee and hosted a night-owl talk show from his car while he cruised the town for impromptu guests and their stories.

Each contingent in Wanda's party had its own vehicle parked in line on the shoulder of the highway. At the head of the line of vehicles was a motorcycle with a sidecar parked facing the wrong direction.

"And Dean," Wanda said summoning a last person who stood apart outside the group.

Dean ignored Wanda's summons, but when I stuck my hand out to him, he stepped forward to shake hands with cameras clanking around his neck and looking like a one-man war in pocket-bulging fatigues and various other gear of several foreign armies. He wore a Palestinian burnoose around his neck, and under his Israeli army beret he was bald with a long kinky ponytail and a full beard.

"Dean's *freelance*," Wanda said winking diagnosis at me.

Dean was the owner of the motorcycle with the sidecar, and it was his strobe-flash, synched to his camera's high-speed motor-drive, that had blinded me mid-jeté. He had been following Wanda's convoy westbound and, seeing a leaping Santa Claus on the other side of the highway, he had cut across the median flashing three frames per second while the others U-turned via the overpass. It was Dean who got to me first and pulled me away from an oncoming car.

After the introductions, Wanda put the beard back on me and organized the three photographers and the TV cameraman into taking their pictures of the Hitchhiking Santa Claus. Wanda was like a movie director setting up shots, calling for camera angles and moves to get the lights of Las Vegas always in the background, telling me where and how to stand, where and how to look and how not to squint into the spotlight of the TV videocam, how to shoulder my duffel more photogenically, even how to stick out my thumb to supposedly passing cars. The camera lights and the passing car lights hurt my eyes. After being blinded by Dean's high-powered flash, my eyes kept watering, burning and blurring the outlines of everything as though I had been swimming in too much chlorine.

While this was going on, the newspaper reporter and the TV reporter stood off-camera barraging me with who-what-where-when-why questions, all of which I refused to answer in case my story reached Kansas City and the family before I did. Wanda enthusiastically abetted my mystery Santa act.

"Don't you love him?" Wanda asked the two reporters. "Or does a great story have to bite you first?" and she teased the newspaper man with a playful pinch in the ass.

"I love him!" the newspaper man yelped. "Do me some more!"

"Later," Wanda flirted.

"I'll rest up," he said, standing up straight to suck in his gut.

"Honey, I won't let you down," she said.

"Promises, promises," he said, letting out his breath and his stomach.

The newspaper man bought my anonymity angle and quit questioning me. The TV reporter, to Wanda's annoyance, would not take the hint and kept pressing me for my name and destination. I identified myself only as Santa Claus on a transcontinental Christmas mission, at liberty to divulge nothing to grown-ups. Then she changed from eager cub reporter to hard-hitting investigative journalist, badgering and goading to provoke me into some inadvertent revelation.

Through it all, the TV camerman never said a word. He was a real pro, silver-haired but athletic and limber, gliding around for shots as though the big videocam on his shoulder were part of him. He began to get silently irritated, though, when he couldn't get any shots of me thumbing an actual passing car because every driver slowed to rubberneck our showbiz at work in the spotlight and the flashbulbs.

After my long day of hoping and praying that cars would stop for me, Las Vegas had me angrily wanting them to keep on going. It was one of those black holes of spinning nightmare logic, classic Wizard. I was sticking my thumb out to cars, doing it to get home, but only for the camera; I did not want a ride and the slowing gawkers did not want to give me a ride. I was headed in the wrong direction, but going nowhere, losing time on a gamble to get home faster and safer, risking worse on the chance for better by pretending to hitch rides I did not want from drivers whose interest only kept me at a standstill.

Again and again we waited in the wind for another approaching car, at which Wanda would direct me to assume my hitching pose while she and everybody else but the cameraman who was filming me, seven of the nine of us, frantically but futilely signaled the driver to maintain speed.

Our group exasperation, aggravated by the cold, showed how easy it is even for professional colleagues to factionalize into ugly mob-majority rule. The squabbling became rancorous when Wanda ordered her photographer to get in the newspaper team's car, back it down the highway, and drive by me for the cameraman. The newspaper reporter said no, it was a company car and, insurance-wise, no one but an employee of the newspaper could drive it. But it was the only anonymous vehicle present—Wanda's car advertised Caesars Palace all over it, the TV van and the radio personality's station wagon were also emblazoned with identification, Dean's motorcycle with sidecar was obviously out of the question—so the newspaper reporter was argued into doing the drive-by himself.

This manipulation of a news story by a journalist offended the TV reporter. Her indignation was ignored. We had to reshoot the drive-by because the first time the newspaper reporter did not back down the road far enough to come past me at realistic speed.

"One more time," the TV cameraman ordered. It was the first time I heard him speak.

"What the hell for?" the TV reporter demanded.

"For art!" he snapped back at her.

Then the brewing catfight erupted between Wanda and the TV reporter, who insisted on filming her close-up interview with me there on the spot. Wanda decided that I would first ride into town with the radio personality and do his live interview, which she said would get us all out of the cold and, more important, foment the human interest of my arrival into newsworthiness.

"*Newsworthiness,*" Wanda repeated to the TV reporter. "Which, you may not know yet, is as rare in Vegas at Christmastime as a married man who stays all night. So if we all get lucky working *together,* a radio-newsworthy traveling Santa Claus might generate a TV-newsworthy welcoming crowd at Caesars."

The TV reporter shook her head. "The point of the story is he's *on the road.* He's the Hitchhiking Santa Claus, or isn't he?"

"On his way to Caesars Palace!" Wanda argued. "The point being, *PLEASE,* for Christ's crying sake, don't film an interview without Caesars in the background! Give credit where credit's due. This is Caesars' party. And anyway wouldn't some nice flashing neon make for a better backdrop than out here?" She gestured at the dark around us and winked at the TV cameraman. "This is almost as boring as making love without mirrors!"

The TV reporter waited for her cameraman and the others to stop chuckling before she announced to Wanda, "Crowd or no crowd, with or without neon, I've got a deadline. Do you want your coverage here and now or not at all? Take it or leave it."

Amused, Wanda opened her coat and put her hands on her hips, showing off her very impressive figure, and answered, "There will be no on-camera interview with Caesars Palace's Santa Claus without Caesars Palace in the background."

Then, while one hand stayed on her hip holding her coat open, Wanda's other hand took possessive hold of me.

"Take it or leave it yourself, sweetie," Wanda said, all smiles.

The TV reporter, who was only a few well-educated years older than I and several feminist years younger than Wanda, was outraged at being called "sweetie."

"How can you? How *dare* you? A fellow woman!" the TV reporter huffed.

"Come on, sweetie," the radio personality chimed in, baiting her, one hand holding his toupee on in the wind while he stamped his feet against the cold. "The rest of us would like to get this show *off* the road."

The TV reporter was already incensed at Wanda, but she went nuclear at being called "sweetie" by a man. "Sweetie" rankled and enraged not only her own whole life, but all the vicarious lives of all the other women who made up her entire intellectual, emotional, and historical conscience. "Sweetie" took her clear back to Eve cursed out of Eden for delivering the news to Adam. I could see the TV reporter as Eve looking back over her shoulder at Paradise through those first human tears and, as Adam stumbles ahead, she raises her arm in farewell to God's evicting angel at the gate and gives him the finger on behalf of all women ever after.

"My cameraman and I are covering a *news story*!" she shouted. "We are *not* making any goddamn commercial for Caesars fucking Palace!"

Her cameraman, hearing this, rolled his eyes and put down his videocam and walked off into the desert to take a leak.

"Suit yourself, sweetie," Wanda said, pulling me away with her arm in mine. "Roy, let's do it!" she shouted, exhorting the radio personality who gratefully picked up my duffel and rushed off down the line of parked vehicles to his station wagon.

Instructing the others to follow us to Caesars, Wanda conducted me to the station wagon. It had radio call letters and Roy's face caricatured on the back and on both sides and on the roof, and a huge antenna attached front and back so it looped high over the entire length of the car.

Roy was already starting the car and turning on the heater as Wanda ushered me to the front passenger door. She crowded in after me and we bumped and bounced together across the seat. I slid way over into the ample middle to give her plenty of room, but she kept on coming, lifting my arm around her shoulders and snuggling as close and tight to me as she could. I could feel her shivering in her coat, which surprised me after her scathing performance with the TV reporter.

Wanda rubbed her hand briskly up and down my thigh and shuddered, "Warm me up, Santa!"

Roy got a blanket out of the backseat and we spread it over our three laps. Wanda returned her hand to my thigh under the blanket while Roy fiddled with the dashboard-mounted switches and dials of his mobile broadcasting unit. He put on a headset microphone and handed another just like it to me. Wanda, enjoying our close quarters, helped me pull off my stocking cap and beard. She dropped them in her lap and put her hand back under the blanket, higher on my thigh. I put on the headset.

Through the windshield we watched the TV reporter and the cameraman arguing over who was going to drive their van. He stood blocking the driver's door and she shoved past him and started to climb in, but he pulled her out, whereupon she glared at him, silently demanding to be unhanded. He let go of her and backed away from her with his hands raised in mock surrender. She got in behind the wheel and slammed the door. The cameraman took his time coming around the rear of the van to the passenger side, lingering to show us that he had the car keys.

"Looks like you're losing film at eleven," Roy said.

"Little bitch," Wanda said, untroubled, squeezing her nearly intimate hold on my thigh. "She knows we're going to hype this thing big big and she doesn't dare go back to her producer without it. Dead news night like this, hell, I can pull the Mayor."

"His Honor!" Roy stentorized, joking; then, impressed with the idea, he asked, "You think?"

"So what's the little bitch going to say? All this film out here and she goes back without *The Mayor Welcoming Santa Claus at Caesars Palace*? Because somebody called her 'sweetie'? Come on, she knows she blew it. She's smart enough to be shitting in her tights right now."

"Assuming His Honor," Roy said. "He's doing the rodeo tonight, handing out World Champeen belt buckles."

"Don't worry about His Honor. Bozo will come running with

his key to the city hanging out. Big media night for him, what with the shitkickers and you, Santa. You're about to go famous."

The TV cameraman finally got in the van and after another moment it peeled out, rooster-tailing dust into the wind. The dust swirled white in our headlights, then darkened into a solid cloud, enclosing the station wagon. Roy poked me in the ribs with his elbow.

"Scared to death, clearly," Roy said, needling Wanda.

"Shitting in her feminist tights, even as we speak," Wanda assured him, electrifying the inside of my thigh with her long fingernails. "*Big,* Santa! *Big* big! Too big for her to live without you!"

Wanda's hand incited an erection that had me blushing, stinging my face back to life from the cold. Other parts of me were beginning to feel the heater, too. Notwithstanding my embarrassment, from discovery of which Wanda was only inches away, it was luxurious relief to be out of the wind sandwiched between warming bodies, cozily encapsulated inside the blowing dust. Wearing the headset in the cockpit glow of the dashboard dials, I felt once more like an astronaut copiloting blind but secure through clouds.

The dust thinned and brightened ahead again and the headlights flickered clear, revealing Dean helmeted, goggled, burnoose-swathed faceless astride his motorcycle—a warrior-escort impervious to the dust and the wind—and I steeled my resolve to make that plane ticket happen. As Roy aimed us at Vegas, coordinating over the mike with the radio station to go on the air at any moment, I tightened my arm around Wanda and gave up worrying about what her spidery fingers soon communicated with under the blanket.

30

I did not hear what my interview sounded like because Roy turned off our radio between commercials; he said the echo-delay of our voices would drive us crazy. During the commercials he kept telling me not to be nervous, to sit back and forget about the mike and just shoot the breeze with him. The motto of Roy's show, which he repeated every time he went back on the air, was, *"Life is a conversation—so talk to me!"*

But I was tongue-tied and still having trouble with my eyes. The lights of Las Vegas, those thousands of fuzzy colors that lay spreading with our approach, were suddenly an audience listening to the strange things Wanda's hand was doing to my voice.

As low-key as I could, faking a troublesome cough to cover a sporadic uncontrollable yodel, I maintained my anonymity and the secrecy of my destination, tried to express my gratitude to Caesars Palace and to the city of Las Vegas for their hospitality, and answered everything else with questions of my own that kept Roy doing most of the talking. Over the years I have survived hostile parents, teachers, cops, girlfriends, intrusive authority in general, by learning how to answer questions with questions.

This technique worked like a charm on Roy. He took my strangeness for mike-fright and answered me with on-the-road anecdotes of his own. Roy's anecdotes let me off the hook, but they also gave me goose bumps because they made such eloquent sense of my squirming gibberish. Listening to him, while Wanda's fingers worked their expertise under the blanket, I was amazed at how interesting it was to be a lonely heroic Santa Claus hitchhiking across America at Christmastime.

Roy was so good, he sold me my own story. I saw why he was such a great success on night-owl radio, which is all about nothing but loneliness. He was a spellbinder who took my loneliness and inspired me with it. His skill at this derived from an extraordinary ability to listen to people and communicate them back to themselves. And like anyone with an extraordinary ability, it made him magical to an audience.

Roy was really like a radio himself; a powerful receiver able to pick up the faintest signals and amplify them out of thin air. If you had a radio like Roy, you could tune in on the whole world. No matter where you were, the air would be full of voices, music, meaning. Silence would speak to you. You could read people's minds, as a good listener always seems to be doing.

When we got into Vegas traffic, other drivers honked at the station wagon and Roy waved back at them. Wanda had me put on my beard and stocking cap and started me waving along with Roy to the honkers. They were our audience. Roy demonstrated this to me by asking them, over the air after they honked, to flash their high beams if they believed in Santa Claus. *"So talk to me!"* Not one honker abstained. Roy described their cars over the air and sent them forth as rolling emissaries to be honked at and high-beamed by other listening drivers who also believed in Santa Claus.

This expanding network of Santa believers so moved Roy that he wanted to involve the rest of our audience, those good people scattered but listening together, as he said, all over Las Vegas and on out across the Great American Desert. So he asked everyone who could hear us, in their cars or homes or on the job or wherever they were, to wait until he counted to three and then welcome Santa Claus to Las Vegas by flashing any light they could for ten seconds.

"Hey, flash your lights and/or honk your horns, anything, just let it rip for ten seconds in that three-beat rhythm of 'Jingle Bells'!"

Before Roy counted to three, though, he elaborated his inspiration to include the farthest-flung members of our audience. He addressed truckers soloing that long winter haul, and anyone else out there on their own way to the other end of the night. Remembering his friends inside the Clark County Jail who had no access to the lights of their cells, he suggested they substitute flashing with flushing in unison. Roy was determined to include every last one of our listeners. If they were lying in bed, their own bed or elsewhere, alone or not, in penthouse suites or claptrap motels, dormitories, barracks, hospitals, incapacitated by illness or age or circumstances, suffering no matter what grief, lying there listening in the dark, he asked them to sing or hum or blink or even just think "Jingle Bells."

"On three, everybody—scattered out there—*ten seconds for Santa Claus!*"

Then at last Roy counted and on three we were suddenly driving through pandemonium. Cars honked, headlights flashed, windows and whole buildings illuminated off and on; people in cars shouted and waved to us, to each other, to people on the street who shouted and waved back even though they were radioless and confused by the joyous riot around them. Under the blanket, Wanda's hand participated in avid "Jingle Bells" rhythm.

Days later I read newspaper accounts of those ten seconds. A hospital nurse reported the eeriness of listening to patients in separate rooms who all at once started singing "Jingle Bells." Cops in the Clark County Jail described their sequential impressions of the toilets flushing as an earthquake, a plane crash, an explosion, a jailbreak. Pipes burst, cells flooded, inmates were without plumbing until late the next afternoon. Clark County officials threatened legal action against Roy and his radio station, but it got laughed away. Two babies, born miles apart during those ten seconds, were both named Nicolas to commemorate our coinciding arrivals. Simultaneously, several couples hoped to have conceived little September Santas of their own.

31

Wanda pulled the mayor, all right. After Roy's radio eloquence and synchronized mass welcome, His Honor, with entourage and Caesars brass, was already regaling the media-mob at the entrance to the hotel when we arrived.

Trying to avoid the traffic jam in the horseshoe drive up to Caesars, Roy entered the exit and got us stuck downwind of the fountain under a deluge pounding the roof, slapsplashing the windshield, cascading the windows, keeping us in the car. Roy turned on the wipers and sat back, unhurried, using the delay as a scoop for our listeners, describing the scene at Caesars for them before anyone else knew we were there.

We looked out at a full-on media event that had Wanda's hand ecstatic under the blanket. Watching through the cataract on the windshield and listening to Roy's graphic version of what we were seeing as the roof drummed and the wipers ticked, I could not believe that all those lights and people were waiting for me. At the brightest center of it all, the mayor stood out among the other suits by virtue of his huge cowboy hat, so brand-new and pristine dazzling white that it seemed to soak up and intensify the media lights; as though the hat, even more than the lights, radiated the glare in which surrounding gawkers squinted or shaded their eyes with their hands.

We were stuck dead still in the very localized heavy downpour, but Wanda finally couldn't wait any longer. We exited the station wagon and made a run for it. Someone yelled, "There he is!" and a sudden continuous barrage of flashbulbs had me seeing stars again. Wanda held my hand tight to her hip and led me zigzagging through a claustrophobic maze of people and into the lights centered around the mayor's white cowboy hat.

Flashbulbs rapid-fired the colors in my eyes and I couldn't see a thing while the mayor welcomed me with a big key to the city. Luckily I didn't have to say anything because the suits from Caesars and the media all whooped and whistled and clapped to encourage and augment the civilians.

Then the circus moved inside Caesars, where, en route to my suite, for two hours, the mayor and I were photographed bracketing what had to be every employee of the hotel, in groups and one by one, uniform by uniform, suits through concierges, cashiers, casino dealers, doormen, bellhops, security guards, maids surprised in the hallway outside my suite, and finally inside the suite, where the mayor and I traded hats for the gag photo that later made us both briefly famous around the world—Santa Claus in the white Stetson shaking hands with the Mayor of Las Vegas, Nevada, USA, wearing my stocking cap.

Alone at last, I immediately explored the living room and the bedroom, searching for the minibar in cabinets and closets, everywhere I could see, but I couldn't find it. My Santa suit looked and smelled like laundry was a good idea, so I phoned housekeeping for a rush job and also asked where the minibar was hidden. The woman chuckled at my question, teased me about the orgy-size jacuzzi I had not yet seen in the bathroom, and directed me out to the mirrored foyer of the suite, where I discovered that one of the mirrors was a door into a whole kitchen with a refrigerator full of drinks.

I commandeered a bottle of champagne and sat in the living room overlooking the lights of Las Vegas, listening to the TV for a weather forecast. I was up high, several floors above the Caesars fountain spraying in the wind. The fountain was beautiful from up there, whipping and flying into spindrift. It had me feeling pleasantly far away from those sprinklers back in Barstow, and looking forward to my jacuzzi with Wanda, who had disappeared with a promise to catch me later. I held my glass up to one eye and laughed, scoping the view through champagne, which gave the world a golden cast.

One of the maids came to get my Santa suit for laundering. I went into the palatial marble bathroom to undress and found Wanda already in the jacuzzi, luxuriating with her eyes closed. She was waiting for me with her own bottle of champagne, I thought, until Dean bobbed up in front of her, took a quick swig from the bottle, and re-submerged. They didn't see me grab a robe and retreat to the bedroom.

Undressing alone was lucky, though, because I was startled to find myself wearing women's panties. It took me a confused moment to figure out that they had to be Sharon's, inside her Levi's when I had mistakenly put them on rushed and panicking in the dark. I tore off the panties and, not knowing what to do with them, stuffed them into a pocket of the Caesars robe. Then it hit me that I had left my own underwear along with my socks in Sharon's bed, and I winced at the thought of her husband discovering them with his big feet.

"First thing in the morning all right?" the maid asked as I handed my clothes to her.

"Sooner, if you can, please. I don't have anything else to wear."

"Right away rush. I'll take care of you."

"Thanks."

And leaving, she said, laughing, "You're my prisoner now, Santa! Better give me all I want for Christmas!"

"Careful what you wish for," I said.

The window overlooking the fountain was fixed so it would slide open only a few inches, through which I poked Sharon's panties until they suddenly disappeared in the wind. I stood there and watched the fountain again and drank some more champagne, wishing that Dean and Wanda would get the hell out of my hot tub. I wandered around the living room and picked up the phone. I was dialing Fred's number in KC when a knock on the door interrupted me.

I opened the door to three very bubbly party girls.

"Hi, are you Santa?"

"George said you were having a party."

"We're your new elves," the third girl said with a British accent.

"In the jacuzzi." I pointed and they followed my thumb into the bedroom, tossing purses on the bed as they passed into the bathroom. Through the bedroom doorway I heard squeals, shoes being kicked off, and saw clothes joining purses on the bed.

I closed the bedroom door, but I could still hear raucous laughing and splashing. I sat on the couch in the living room and turned the TV up loud. The local news was boring. I switched to CNN and saw Santa Claus, and after a moment gagged on my champagne, suddenly realizing that I was looking at myself.

I was there on CNN in front of Caesars, being welcomed by the mayor with the key to city—as it had happened, but cinematically and emotionally heightened by crowd-reaction shots of enraptured children watching, *believing* in Santa Claus, wide-eyed and open-mouthed and sharing their wonder with laughing parents. Fred later got a cassette copy of the newsfilm, which ended on a close-up of Wanda's nemesis, the local TV reporter, doing the coverage for CNN. It was her big break, a local story giving her what TV reporters call "national face-time." Apparently she had changed her mind about showbiz journalism, because she was decked out in a red and white stocking cap like mine.

"No telling yet where he's headed," the reporter says, smiling into the camera, swinging her stocking cap as she glances over her shoulder at the crowd around the mayor and me in the background. "The anonymous hitchhiking Santa Claus refuses to identify himself or his destination, saying only that he is, quote, 'on a transcontinental Christmas mission, at liberty to divulge nothing to grownups.' Tonight he is the grateful guest of Caesars Palace and the children of Las Vegas. We'll be following his progress and keep you posted. I'm Susan Lynne, reporting from Las Vegas."

"Wonderful, Suzie," the CNN anchor says, watching from his on-air desk in Atlanta, "just wonderful. Those little faces are what Christmas is all about."

"Honk if you believe in Christmas!" Suzie laughs, still on-camera and loving it.

"*Beep beep,*" the anchor guy quips back at her. "We'll keep checking in with you."

"*Beep beep,*" Suzie says signing off.

Alone on-air from Atlanta, the anchor says, "*Beep beep,* indeed. We're with you, Santa. Good luck to you. He's going to need it if that polar storm front catches him on the road. We'll have continuing updates on those travel advisories througout the Midwest. And stay tuned for CNN's continuing *Santa Watch.*"

"*STAY TUNED!!!*" George Talarian yelled behind me, startling me with his sudden presence, still wearing his yellow-tinted glasses.

I killed the TV volume to say, "We gotta talk, George."

"I got you a plane ride to Kansas City."

"Bless you, George."

"Out of Atlantic City."

"Atlantic City! New Jersey?"

"Guaranteed. Xmas Eve."

"Christmas Eve? Christmas Eve is two days away, George."

"You made CNN! And not just a news pop. They grabbed it into goddam *SANTA WATCH*! Megadream jackpot! Not to mention the network affiliates and all the expanding local TV and radio. You're tomorrow's front page on every rag in town. Human interest, Santa! For the next two days, you are *GOLD*! More important, whatever you touch for the next three days *turns* to gold."

"What airline?"

"Yours, Santa. It's a private plane. Belongs to a friend."

"Who?"

"He owns a place like this in Atlantic City. Most grateful friend you'll ever have in your life. You arrive with your Santa magic on Xmas Eve very, very publicly, and depart privately for Kansas City at hoopla's's end. Guaranteed."

"So I'm supposed to be this kind of crazy Santa hobo hitchhiking into the dead of winter trying to get to . . . Atlantic City?"

George went into pitch-mode. " 'Where is Santa headed? No one knows. Stayed tuned. Where is he today? Stay tuned! Santa's out there in the snow somewhere . . . on his way to someone somewhere the long way, the cold hard way . . . lost out there without his reindeer in a Christmas blizzard. Where, oh, where is Santa Claus? STAY TUNED!!!' "

"Where am I, George?"

"Tomorrow night, you show up—*miraculous*—at one of my grateful friend's other hotels.

"Where, George?"

"Does it matter? Chicago."

"Chicago!"

"Maybe New Orleans."

"That's two-four-five thousand miles!"

"Miraculous!"

"Hitchhiking through an arctic blizzard?"

"Hell no. My friend's corporate jet wings us over the weather."

"Us?"

"Your gig. My show."

"Why don't you just get yourself a Santa suit, George?"

"I don't like to mention it, but the gig doesn't depend at all on you, does it? Like they say, the clothes make the man."

"I could go on TV and take off the beard. Throw myself on the mercy of my public. Blow the whistle on your public-relations scam."

George wagged a warning finger at me and said, "Oops. All my grateful friends would not like that. Besides, who is scamming whom here? Or what the hell do *you* call traveling around at Xmastime in a Santa Claus suit?"

"On the other hand, I could just say no."

"Little late for that," George said, gesturing ominously around the suite. "Take a lesson from the weather, kid. It's getting dangerous. Pay attention to those travel advisories. Don't let people down. Time to take your act seriously . . . and ride it home while it's still yours."

"I have to get to Kansas City, George."

"You will. Guaranteed. Xmas Eve. Meanwhile, your hot tub runneth over." He left me sitting there while he went into the kitchen.

"Wanda's already in there with a photographer and your three friends," I called to him.

"Guy's outnumbered," George said and headed for the party with more champagne and two bottles of cognac.

3²

T̶hrough the bedroom door I caught a glimpse of one of George's girls, naked and shining wet, out of the hot tub only long enough to turn on a CD player at maximum volume. While the music pounded through the suite, I sat there on the couch looking down on the fountain, brain racing for an escape from this, the Wizard's latest brilliant recovery from worse to worse.

Jackpot George had turned as threatening as the weather, and I didn't even have my clothes. All I could think of was to steal George's clothes, get out of there, and call Fred. Reconnoitering first, though, I checked outside the suite and found a security guard stationed in the hallway. Seeing me, he stood up.

"Hey there, Santa."

"How're you doing out here? Can I get you a drink or something?"

"That's mighty nice of you, but no thanks."

"You hungry?"

"I'm fine. But you live it up. Try that room service."

"Are we making too much noise?"

"I'll say. But don't worry about it. You and your friends have the whole floor to yourselves."

"Come to the party."

"No can do." But hearing a sudden loud female surge of hot-tub fun inside the suite, he checked his watch and said, "Maybe later, if you're still at it."

"You can hear we need a lifeguard."

I closed the door on him and slowly, silently locked and chained it, convinced that he was there more to keep me from going anywhere than he was to protect me from being mobbed by Santa fans. I filled my champagne glass and went into the kitchen, picked up the phone, and dialed Fred's number.

A hotel operator came on the line. "I'm sorry, but calls on this line have been restricted. May I help you?"

"Can you make it collect, please? Person-to-person, please, to Frederica Rickert."

"Santa Claus calling?

"No! Please! Please just say it's Casey."

Fred's recorded message answered, then Fred's voice interrupted and she accepted the call.

"Casey! You all right?"

I was so glad to hear her voice that I couldn't speak.

"Casey?"

"I'm here."

"What's wrong?"

"I . . ."

"Tell me."

"I'm sorry I missed that plane."

"It's OK. It wasn't OK at the time. As your father likes to say, *'The excrement impacted with the whirling electrical appliance.'* But I played your very amazing message to him, and it's OK now."

"What did he say about med school?"

"He told me he wouldn't want to write your malpractice insurance." She laughed and started to cry.

I choked on a laugh and tried not to let her hear me weeping along with her. "I'm sorry to let you down, Fred. And not be there for Matt."

"Matt's having a hard time, a real hard time without his papa. We both are. We need you, Casey. But you never let me down. You just always make things so hard on yourself. It's always win or crash for you. I mean . . . *extra credit for dissecting a human heart . . . ?* Davy would love it."

"You think?"

"Win or crash. He told me once that your life is like an opera where the corpse won't stop singing."

"Davy said that?"

"He admired you. He argued with your father all the time about you. 'Moth to the flame, hell,' he'd answer the old man, 'Casey's a moth to the *moon.*'

"Poor Dad. He lost the wrong son."

"Your father sells insurance! Disasters are bad for business, and you're always bringing one home."

"And he hates opera."

"Yeah, he likes that cowboy music where everybody's crying in their beer."

"Dad and Davy, both."

"All those songs about bars and lost love at closing time."

"I know, give me a break."

"Give me a beer!"

And, as always, we had each other laughing.

"So listen up, old friend," Fred said. "The most important thing for all of us right now is to keep you from flunking out of college. You just stick to your guns and do what you have to do. You missed that plane, but I fixed your ticket so it's still good."

"Uh . . . Fred?"

"Let me know when to pick you up."

"Fred?"

"Yeah?"

I could not bring myself to disappoint her with the truth, and said, "Can I talk to Matt?"

"He's not here. He's over at your house."

"Without you?"

"You remember how sad he was about his birthday. Well, Christmas was even worse until, all of a sudden today, he went absolutely bananas over this crazy guy who's hitchhiking across the country dressed up as Santa Claus."

"What!"

"'The Hitchhiking Santa Claus.' He's all over the news. Won't tell anybody his name or where he's going. They made a big deal out of him tonight in Las Vegas. Mayors all over the country are inviting him to their cities. Competing for him, even, like he's the Olympics or a convention. Reporters are really milking it. Some of the man-in-the-street interviews are hilarious. It's the first time anyone ever thought about what they would give Santa Claus for Christmas. Everybody's getting in on it, hoping they'll see him.

There's a contest for kids to guess his destination, so your father got Matt a big map of America and the two of them are glued to the TV, determined, in my angelic little Matt's words, 'To track that sucker and score the trip to Disney World.' "

"Dad's interested, too?"

"You know your father. He says the guy's a wacko, but he admires the PR hype and he says Matt will at least learn some geography. Deep down, though . . ."

"What?"

"This hitchhiking Santa Claus has really lit a Christmas fire under Matt . . . and it's nice to see your father warming up with him."

I was so amazed I forgot to talk.

"Casey, you there?"

"Yeah. Fred, I better get off now. These people are waiting for me."

"We're waiting for you, too. But don't worry. Just get it done. Don't worry about anything else. And then we'll celebrate. I've got plans for you and me on New Year's Eve. Take care, baby."

"Take care."

I hung up the phone in a daze. Being anonymously famous—*and to my father!*—felt like I had a secret power suddenly under control, like waking into a dream that was all the more strange for being so familiar. I stood in the kitchen and drank my champagne, tasting it carefully, feeling the bubbles, my mind for once an absolute blank.

33

$\mathcal{M}$*y empty glass* brought me out of the kitchen for a refill. In the living room I found one of the girls, the one with the British accent, sitting on the couch wearing nothing but a towel. Her purse was open beside her and she was busy studying the question cards from a game of Trivial Pursuit. She had a glass of champagne and, filling mine, she was too drunk to keep from missing her aim.

"Sorry," she said. "I needed a breather. Wanda gets to be a bit much."

"Are you a Trivial Pursuit expert?"

"I loathe the game," she said, "but the cards are a really good way to learn about America."

"What a great idea."

"You think so?"

"Yeah. Take away the game and they're flash cards. Information. Brilliant."

Her eyes were sleepy and sad even when she smiled. "At least, they help me get your jokes."

"For instance?"

"Oh, I don't know."

"No, please. Tell me one."

"Well, for instance, do you know why an Eskimo—no matter how hungry he is, and even if his children are starving—will never eat a penguin?"

"Because an Eskimo lives at the North Pole and penguins live at the South Pole."

"I guess everybody knows that one."

"No, I go to college . . . and all we do is play Trivial Pursuit."

"You're a good egg." She laughed, but her eyes stayed sad. She looked toward the bedroom door and, clutching the towel more or less around her, slid closer to me on the couch. Her intention, though, was not what I thought. "You're in trouble here, college boy, do you know?"

"George Talarian."

"All snakes have yellow eyes."

"What's the fear of snakes called?"

"Ophidiophobia."

"Hey, you're good."

"George and Wanda want to get another Santa Claus to go to Chicago and Atlantic City or wherever else. They don't want you to talk to anybody and ruin their show."

"What'll they do with me?"

"They haven't decided. George wants to take you for a long ride out in the desert and feed you to the weather. Wanda says to get you arrested for vagrancy and lose you in jail until you don't matter. You'll be just another 'John Doe.' These are bad eggs, college boy."

"Telling me this could be dangerous for you."

She smiled at me, sleepy drunk, and said, "I'm bad, too."

"I really don't think so."

She let go of the towel and it fell away as she coiled her arms around my neck. "Want to see how bad I can be? Tell me, what is the condemned man's last wish?"

I extricated gently from her arms. "I really don't think so . . . what's your name?"

"Sandy. Why not?"

"You're a good egg, Sandy."

Just then the doorbell buzzed and a key opened the door, but whoever it was couldn't get in past the chain. The doorbell kept buzzing while I got up and went to answer it. I peeked through the door and saw the maid with my laundered Santa Claus suit and other clothes on hangers inside a plastic bag.

"Hey, that was fast. I can't thank you enough."

I heard the maid talking to someone as I closed the door to unlock the chain and, opening the door wide enough to take the clothes, I saw that she was accompanied by a little girl, shy and excited, clutching an autograph book and a pen. The security guard was still sitting in his chair.

The maid stepped in front of the little girl to block her view of me in my robe and, closing the door just open enough to talk to me, said, "Could I ask you a favor?"

"Name it."

"My little niece here would be so grateful for Santa's autograph."

"I'll tell him," I said. "Where can he find you?

"Just down the hall."

"Right away rush."

She took the little girl's hand and they walked away, and I gave the security guard a friendly thumb's-up as I closed the door.

I took off the robe and got dressed right there in the foyer. I knew it was going to be cold outside so I put the robe back on over my sweatshirt and Levi's and tucked it into the baggy pants of the Santa suit, then put on the Santa coat and the stocking cap. Cleaned up, the Santa Claus suit looked so good that I went into to the kitchen and got the beard to check out the whole effect. Back in the foyer, the surrounding mirrors multiplied me into an infinite army of well-dressed Santas.

Sandy, having abandoned the formality of her towel, was waiting for me on the couch. Seeing me in full Santa regalia, though, she instinctively covered herself, like a child being good.

"Do you want to save Santa Claus?" I asked her.

"How?"

"There's a security guard out in the hall. Get him into the hot tub."

Sandy grinned with those sad eyes I'll never forget and said, "No problem."

She stood and wrapped the towel around her, filled her champagne glass, and we headed out through the foyer.

"Get Wanda's clothes and that photographer's clothes out of the bathroom," I said, "and put them on the bed with all the others. Hide yours separate. And close the bathroom door."

I went into the kitchen to wait. Immediately, there was a knock and it was Sandy.

"What?" I asked.

Without saying anything, she kissed me and turned to her mission while I reclosed the kitchen door.

It didn't take her long to get the guard to join the party. Sandy made sure I heard them come in, and when I came out of the kitchen there was a trail of the guard's clothes into the bedroom. I picked up the clothes and tossed them on the couch, went into the bedroom and grabbed my cowboy boots, and gathered all the clothes on the bed and took them out to the living room.

I stuffed the clothes through the narrow opening of the window overlooking the fountain, and the wind took them flying away into the night. The weight of the security guard's gun holstered to his belt took his trousers in a straight drop.

Then, carrying my boots and my duffel, I hurried out through the mirrors in the foyer and down the hall to where the maid was waiting with her little niece.

Seeing me pull on my boots over bare feet, the little girl whose name was Agatha looked up at her aunt and said, "Santa's a cowboy."

3⁴

Things were getting worse quite nicely. Flunking out of college was a snap compared to Vegas bad guys with guns and jail and killer weather. But after everything Fred had told me about the Hitchhiking Santa Claus, as well as having seen some of it firsthand on CNN, I knew I couldn't just blow the whistle on George Talarian's scam. Neither could I let him get away with it by ditching the Santa suit and simply walking away as my anonymous self. I kept thinking of all those kids caught up in it like Matt, and the look in little Agatha's eyes when she saw me. Not to mention even my father trying to map my destination.

It pissed me off how corny my new dilemma was: Not only did I have to get myself out of deepening trouble, but now I had to save Santa Claus, too.

I left Caesars as publicly as I could, stepping out of the elevator with Agatha in my arms and her aunt beside us.

It was Agatha who had the most fun that night as we crossed

the casino and people waved and yelled and crowded after us. Cowboys around a crap game doffed their hats and yahooed us. Other gamblers quit tables and slot machines to join our slow, crowd-impeded passage, monitored by security guards conferring on their walkie-talkies.

The crowd followed us outside and down the horseshoe drive past the fountain blowing in the wind. On the sidewalk, the TV reporter was pulling on her Santa hat as she intercepted us in the light of her cameraman filming. She told me we were on live to CNN and stuck her microphone in my face. I waved to the camera, kissed Agatha and put her in her aunt's arms, kissed her aunt, and, live on CNN, walked out into the middle of the Strip and raised my thumb to the traffic jam I was causing.

"EAST!" I yelled, "ANYBODY GOING EAST! I'M LOOKING FOR EAST!"

Drivers laughed and shouted destinations, and I became an auctioneering Santa Claus, "NO THANK YOU, WINNEMUCCA! . . . NO THANK YOU, LA!!! I NEED EAST!!! WHO'LL GIVE ME EAST!!! THANK YOU, KINGMAN!!! DO I HEAR ALBUQUERQUE!!!"

Police sirens wailed out of the distance while I beseeched the cars blocking the Strip. Up in the window of my suite, I saw George Talarian and the security guard watching, hiding their nakedness behind the window curtains. Wanda peered out from behind George, so he seemed to have two heads. He grabbed a walkie-talkie away from the security guard. As I worked the crowd, adrenalizing from determined to desperate, a hand on my shoulder startled me silent.

I turned and looked, looked up, way up at a man who I later learned was a full-blooded Hopi Indian cowboy, close to seven feet tall, and so massive that no one probably ever expressed anything but admiration for his cascading crow-black hair that had never been cut in all his thirty-odd years and was as long as I am tall.

"I'll take you where you need to go," the Indian said to me.

I followed him to his car, which, without the mud covering it, would have been identifiable as a once-silver Lincoln Continental over ten years old. The trunk was too full of stuff to close, secured with rope. He crammed my duffel into the backseat with a saddle and tack and ropes and other rodeo cowboy equipment, loose clothes, lanterns, and camping gear. Opening the passenger door, I found the seat occupied by what took me a moment to realize was a curled-up baby reindeer only a few weeks old.

"Get in," the Indian said. "She'll shift."

I made space for myself, easing the little reindeer down between my knees and somewhat in my lap. The Indian gunned the engine to part the crowd and everybody waved laughing and cheering as the Continental clattered slowly away on only four sick cylinders. Sirens arrived behind us and I looked back at the traffic jam clearing, leaving the cops mystified by a problem that had disappeared.

Even without the mechanical decrepitude of the car, I was apprehensive at the prospect of riding twelve hundred miles with a baby reindeer between my legs.

Shaking hands with me, the Indian said, "Langford Tuwalakum."

"Is that an Indian expression?"

"It's my name."

I apologetically shook his hand again. "Casey."

"Lang."

Silence. Trying to make conversation, I scratched the little reindeer and asked, "Who is this?"

"Soyal."

" 'Soyal.' Uh-huh."

"It's an Injun name. Hopi. Means 'Returning.' She's a Christmas present for my kids."

"Where's home?"

"Most of the year I rodeo and home's where I send the checks. My kids live on the reservation with their mama."

"You must miss them."

"Like I'm swimmin' through life with my arms cut off. But their mama's remarried. And I can't save so much money for 'em doin' anything else. Where's your family?"

"Kansas City."

"Long way."

"Seems to get farther and farther."

"Dressed up like Santa Claus . . ."

"It's a long story."

"Slows you down."

"You know it."

"I hear you, brother. You're talkin' to an Injun who's a cowboy. Home, hell. Home is where it don't matter how you get there."

"Can't thank you enough for helping me out."

"You don't have to thank me, Santa. My kids will. They saw you on TV and now they're glued to CNN. Watchin' the news of the world waitin' to hear about you."

The Continental did not inspire confidence, clanking along at its top speed of about thirty mph.

"Uh, Lang . . . about going all the way to Kansas City?"

"Not in *this* car."

35

We drove to MacCarran Airport, skirting the public terminal out to the smaller outlying runways, past a sign that said "OWNERS ONLY" into a parking lot where the Continental cruised clicking to a stop in the farthest darkest corner away from a row of private planes.

"Which one's yours?" I asked.

"Wait here," Lang answered as he got out and I watched him Indian off into the dark toward the planes.

I couldn't believe my luck, to be flying home after all. I was so happy I kissed the reindeer. The weight of her had put my legs to sleep. Needing to uncramp, I opened the door and lifted my legs over the reindeer and hauled myself out, hanging on to the car while my legs tingled back to life.

Waiting for Lang, I freed my duffel from the jumble in the backseat and dropped it ready on the ground. Still waiting, scratching the reindeer, I found a baby bottle half full of milk on the floor of the car. I was feeding the reindeer, humming "Jingle Bells" to her, when I was startled again by Lang's big hand on my shoulder.

"Let's fly," he said.

Lang picked up the reindeer and carried her around his neck, leading me out among mostly corporate jets and other high-rent airware to a small prop plane, just big enough for a baby reindeer to ride behind Santa Claus and his giant Indian pilot. Boarding, I was impressed by the difference between the well-kept plane and Lang's rolling wreck of a Continental.

"Nice," I said. "Traveling so much, you're smart not to throw away money on a car."

While I stowed my duffel and got settled in the copilot's seat, Lang fiddled with wires under the instrument panel. I saw sparks.

"Is there a problem?"

"Can't find the damn key."

Lang hotwired the engine alive and we taxied lurching out onto a runway. Lang got on the radio and traded pilot lingo with the control tower, who seemed as confused as I was by his mumbojumbo but OK'd him for takeoff. Crosswinds slammed us sideways as Lang accelerated, over-revving down the runway.

"Have we got your flight plan?" the voice on the radio asked.

"Roger," Lang answered. "How's the weather monster?"

"Big and fast. Salt Lake's closed. Denver's about to close, advising alternates as far south as Phoenix and Albuquerque. You're going to be racing a train—a *Polar Express*."

"Let her buck. Out." Lang let the mike drop as we bounced along, skewing airborne. "Weather's for civilians," he said to me. "I was in the Air Force."

"What did you fly?"

"Ground crew. We joyrode everything we got our wrenches on."

The plane bucked. I tightened my seat belt. Finding myself in yet another wild ride over which I had no control, I closed my eyes and took my deep diver's breath.

"Wish we had an AM radio," Lang said.

Glad for something to do, I dug my Walkman out of my duffel and unplugged the earphones to externalize music.

"Great, but save the batteries for weather news."

I turned off the Walkman and looked out the window. Las Vegas receded without sinking behind us.

"Aren't we flying a little low?" I asked.

"Wish I could take you the scenic route farther north over the Grand Canyon. Hopi Reservation's close and we could buzz my kids. It'd knock their socks off to see their dad piloting Santa Claus. But flyin' dark with that storm out there, I figure we'll just follow I-40 east and turn north at Oklahoma City. Safety first."

"Right."

"Or we can cut the corner wherever we are at first light."

"Right."

"Worse comes to worse, we can set her down on the interstate and taxi clear to Kansas City."

"Safety first," I nodded, nervously reassured by what I took for sensible flight assessment from an experienced pilot. Then I looked at the instrument panel and froze in staring terror.

"Lang?"

"What?"

I reached out and turned on the plane's factory-equipped radio. "This isn't your plane, is it?"

"Not on the ground."

I covered my face with my hands.

"But don't worry."

"Why not, Lang? Why not worry?"

"We've got plenty of gas."

36

We flew southeast until we picked up I-40, then followed it, bucking crosswinds, zigzagging so low that I was able to read the highway signs. I watched dark desert give way to pine forest as the interstate wound toward Flagstaff. To distract myself from how close we were to the treetops, I dug *Deliverance* and the McDonald's bag of cherry pies out of my duffel. I gave a cherry pie to Lang and we bumped along munching.

"Have you always lived a life of crime, Lang?"

"Used to ride with a motorcycle gang. You ever been to Gallup, New Mexico, on a Saturday night?

"No. Tough town?"

"Every Saturday night, Custer dies again. We called ourselves the Organ Donors."

"And reincarnated as spare parts."

"Not *our* organs. *Yours,* if you messed with us. But all that changed when my kids come."

"What are their names?"

"My boy's Harley Davidson Tuwalakum."

"Good name."

"My little girl's Sara Poli."

"Pretty."

"Poli is Hopi for 'Butterfly.' "

"Do you know that Sara means 'Princess?' "

"Now, hey. 'Princess Butterfly.' That's her, exactly. 'Princess Butterfly.' Thanks for tellin' me that. It's a gift. Uh-oh."

Suddenly we were flying blind through fog. Lang descended until the fog wisped thin and thick and, through it, I saw treetops rushing by on both sides. We were hurtling thirty feet above the ground through a canyon of trees, following the interstate's winding climb back into the fog. I watched the trees disappear, looked down, and saw the ground rising as Lang descended for visibility. The ground disappeared and the plane hit hard. Lang throttled back fast and we went into a skid, but held the road and taxied on up the four-lane. Lang let out a yahoo.

"YES!" I shouted, "WELL DONE!"

We taxied, climbing blind, the fog around us aglow with our blinking green and red and white running lights. Lang kept the plane centered on the faint glimpses of broken line dividing lanes. Suddenly we tipped forward into descent. The fog thinned, gradually revealing the highway.

A dropping curve opened a straight stretch between trees, the end of it lost in dark, and Lang accelerated down the chute for takeoff. Picking up speed, the plane's headlight revealed no more road as we approached the curve too fast to take it on the ground. At the last hopeless moment, Lang pulled us aloft and the plane swooped banking inside the wall of trees. Yahooing our heads off at our shared survival, we ascended over I-40 and Lang pointed to the lights of Flagstaff in the distance ahead.

"Flagstaff's clear. Gonna get real boring now till sunup. I'm gonna grab a snooze."

He let go of the controls and I grabbed the wheel in front of me. "What do I do?"

"You're doin' it," Lang said. "Just keep her level with your hands and turn her with your feet." Watching me, he chuckled at my death grip on the wheel. "Fool around and get the feel of her."

He put the plane into a dive and let me over-recover, pulling the nose up into a stall. The sound of the engine going silent terrified me, but Lang showed no need or desire to take the controls.

"Nose her over," he told me. "Harder."

I pitched the nose back into a dive and the engine miraculously restarted, then I pulled the nose back up, gently this time, until we were flying level. Lang climbed into the backseat with the reindeer and pulled his cowboy hat down over his face.

"How 'bout some music?" he said under his hat.

"What do you like?"

"Up here there ain't nothin' but cowboys."

I tuned in the clearest country-and-western station I could find.

37

Flagstaff floated past, an island of lights in a sea of dark. We flew so close I could see Christmas decorations. The stars were clear and we continued on, following the smaller clusters of lights strung along I-40.

We passed over little towns and roadside businesses and isolated gas stations, all somehow decked out for the holidays. The running lights on our wingtips were Christmas colors, too; red to port, green to starboard.

Two hours or so after Flagstaff, Albuquerque was a huge sprawl of lights, momentous in the dark. I saw running lights of other planes over the airport south of the city, and considered circling north away from them. But I remembered mountains I would not be able to see to the east, so I stayed low and followed the interstate all the way through Albuquerque and out into the dark again. Later I recognized Tucumcari's long straight neon glare of motels along the highway. Over Amarillo I thought about veering northeast over all that Texas flatland, but I-40 was still the only thing I could see. I stayed with it until I saw the glow of Oklahoma City ahead, then cut the corner and picked up I-35 due north.

Lang slept the whole way and I forgot he was there. I listened to the radio. The endless dark and the drone of the prop were like a dream, like infinity broken up into cowboy songs. Like America broken up into all those lights, into all those lives that were then broken up into . . . what?

Flying that plane I figured out that my big brother, David Crockett Rickert, lived 10,681 days. This came out to $46.81 a day in life insurance, which paid Fred double because the old man wrote Davy such a good policy. Accidental death can be a gold mine.

It was a garbage disposal, of all things, that killed Davy. He was helping a friend install it, having a good time, and each thought the other had shut off the electricity. Water was leaking. Davy was wet and grabbed a live wire. He died instantly. One minute he was laughing with his head under a kitchen sink, then suddenly he was gone.

When I was born, the old man bought me a life insurance policy that was now paying my way through college. Somewhere over nowhere that night, it hit me that my father would clean up if I crashed that plane. My final screwup would have an upside. But the downside was even worse than usual, because this time I would also be killing Santa Claus.

It was as though, instead of Davy, *I* was the one who was now the ghost—a live ghost trapped in the identity of this world-famous nonexistent person who brought out the worst and the best in people. George Talarian was like shaking hands with the devil.

Langford Tuwalakum was an atoning angel, trying to do something, even if it was criminal, that would make him a hero to his kids. Where was I? The night before I was stuck up an avocado tree. Twenty-four hours later I had escaped sybaritic corruption and was now doing a couple hundred miles an hour at fifteen hundred feet—a ghost flying with a Hopi Indian cowboy angel and a reindeer.

38

Over Kansas I lost the stars and it started to rain. The lighted ribbon of highway blurred in lowering, thickening clouds. I was never so glad to see Wichita, where I angled northeast to follow the last two hundred miles of Turnpike to Kansas City.

The dark ahead was just turning gray when it started to rain harder. I felt Lang's hand on my shoulder and corrected course as his hand directed, closer east. Looking over my shoulder, I saw Lang too big for the cramped rear seat, feeding the baby bottle to the reindeer on his lap. The plane bucked and kept on bucking and suddenly I was fighting the controls while Lang, bashed around by the turbulence, muscled himself into the pilot's seat.

"Here she comes," he said.

The rain hit harder. Wind shear smashed us into a drop.

"Let's see if we can climb over it."

Lang ascended into cloud the color of wet cement, so dense that the wings and even the prop disappeared. The rain quit, but the buffeting increased. The reindeer panicked. I reached back to calm her and either she jumped or was thrown into my arms. I lifted her into my lap and held her tight to keep her still while we climbed through the deafening violence being done to the plane.

Suddenly it all stopped, the pounding and the noise, and the cabin filled with sunlight as we topped out of the low leading edge of the storm. Under us the top of the cloud cover was endless white, an eerie version of arctic snowfields. Thunderheads, rosy golden white in first light, towered all around us. Lang banked gently back and forth through the maze of billowing behemoths, the most beautiful sight I have ever seen.

"So beautiful," Lang agreed, "and so deadly. The Hopis believe these thunderheads are gods and they're our brothers. Makes sense when you think that nobody can treat you worse than family. You got any brothers?"

And at that moment, looking up at the thunderheads, I finally found a fitting image for what Davy always meant to me.

"Not on the ground," I said.

The reindeer calmed in my arms and went to sleep while we threaded through the thunderheads. One lofted more slender than the others, and Lang made a complete circle around it for me. After a while the thunderheads closed in and Lang began to bank more steeply as our passage narrowed and tightened, but I was still lost in awe.

"Another Hopi deal," I heard him say, "is that we use the colors for our compass. West is the blue-green of the juniper. South is the red of blood. North, the yellow of the Pole Star. East . . ." He directed my gawking attention dead ahead, where the snowy thunderheads joined into a solid insurmountable wall. ". . . is white. The weather monster."

"Oh, shit."

"At least."

Lang put the plane into steep descent. The wall came up at us fast and solid and I expected impact, but we plunged back into shake-rattle-and-roll hell. The cockpit went dark. The reindeer writhed awake and I held tiny flailing hooves.

"I'm watchin' our altitude!" Lang yelled. "Tell me anything you see!"

We plummeted blind, Lang calling out our rapidly decreasing altitude. Suddenly I saw particles hitting the windscreen.

"Snow, Lang!"

"I gotta pull up!"

I saw something else through the snow.

"Wait!"

"Can't! We're too low!"

Lang pulled up hard and steep back into the cement mixer.

"What'd you see!"

"The ground, I think!"

Lang put us back in a dive for another look, calling out our altitude while I peered through the snow barraging the windscreen. I thought I saw something just as Lang pulled up again.

"Can't tell!"

"We're losin' lift! Icing!"

Lang descended again and this time I saw lights through the driving snow. In miraculous irony, we were about to crash into Country Club Plaza, which was decorated, as it is every year at

Christmastime, with thousands and thousands of white lights. Lang saw the lights and pulled us up in time.

"My God," I said, "we're only a couple miles from my house!"

"How big's your yard?"

"The Country Club! Golf course!"

"Where?"

Following my directions, Lang swooped us back dangerously low over the Plaza and I saw the lights again through the snow. Then my neighborhood swept rising under us.

"There!

"Got it!" Lang said and banked hard into final no-choice crash-landing approach. The seventeenth fairway, blanketed with snow, came up too fast ahead. "We're gonna hit hard!"

"There's a deep sand trap on the left!"

Lang corrected and I held the reindeer as we hit in a long sliding horizontal crash that ripped off the wings. I remember the fuselage breaking in two and the cockpit rolling over and over, then suddenly nothing.

39

I **opened my eyes** in a soft gloom. It was quiet and I felt no pain, and it calmly occurred to me that I was dead. Then I saw hands clearing away the gloom, which seemed to be a coffin of snow. The hands wrenched open my coffin, and it was Davy who reached in and took the reindeer out of my arms. Then he pulled me out and we were laughing at this giant snowball from which he had extricated me. Snow was falling, covering us both, and I was so happy to be with Davy. He put the white beard on me and straightened my stocking cap, then I shouldered my duffel and he slung the reindeer around his neck, and we trudged off through the falling snow. I looked back and saw the snow filling our footsteps.

We walked home together, taking all our secret neighborhood shortcuts, knee-deep in snow. Davy hung back as I crunched up across the lawn to the house and rang the doorbell. Waiting, I turned and beckoned Davy to the shelter of the portico. We were both covered with snow. Davy just smiled and nodded and stayed where he was, standing out in the yard with the reindeer around his neck, lifting his open mouth to catch falling snow on his tongue.

My father opened the door. Behind him, I saw my mother and Matt and Fred, all in their pajamas. My father didn't recognize the snow-covered Santa Claus ringing his doorbell, but Fred did and shoved through to throw her arms around me. Matt stared, not knowing what had possessed his mother to embrace a stranger so passionately.

In Fred's arms, I pulled off the beard to reveal myself to my father. "It's me," I heard myself say to him.

My father shook his head in disbelief, then nodded at me and said, "It damn well better be."

"And look who's here," I said turning to summon Davy.

But no one was there.